MW01046979

The Little Sisters of Little Bethel

by

Alice May Bookout

Alice May Bookout

This is a work of fiction. Any resemblance of any of the characters to persons living or dead is strictly coincidental.

FIRST EDITION

UNIVERSITY EDITIONS, Inc.
1905 Madison Avenue
Huntington, West Virginia 25704

Cover by Joan Waites

CONTENTS

INTRODUCTION

On the evening of Friday, September 20, 1985, I stopped at Little Bethel Church which is located near Meadowville in Barbour County, West Virginia. Little Bethel is the oldest church in Barbour County and is Primitive or Old School Baptist. The church was established in 1795, destroyed by a tornado in 1944, and rebuilt on the same site in 1946. In the graveyard accompanying the church are the graves of a Revolutionary War soldier and several from the Civil War. These more recent graves are located toward the front of the graveyard while those toward the back appear to be older. Those in the back of the cemetery have been marked by simpler stones indicating that they are either older or marking the graves of less prosperous persons. Many of the stones in the back of the cemetery have been removed and thrown across the fence dividing the cemetery from pasture and woods. Sunken ground is all that remains of the old grave sites.

I have been drawn to this spot for a number of years but had never taken time to stop. This evening I stopped and mourned the passing of young children. There are many graves of young children, as in any old graveyard. Many women lie beneath the sod in Little Bethel Graveyard. The presence of the Revolutionary War veteran indicates antiquity as we have been wont to count time here in the United States. One of the things that bothers me tonight is the number of stones which appear to be grave markers which have been thrown over the fence. I feel pressure and oppression. What is this place trying to tell me? Why have I been attracted here?

A song came to mind and as I sang it was clear that this was an Indian song and that the spot had been used by Indians. The church was built on an ancient site. The following writings are a result of opening myself to the feelings and spirits in that graveyard.

The Little Sisters of Little Bethel

Friday Evening at Little Bethel

It is cold here in the cemetery. I can feel the coldness of the grave all about me and the wind sighing through the dry autumn leaves. The distant mountains rise bluely against a lighter blue sky. The sounds of humanity are near yet distant. Crickets call slowly through the cool grass. The world is active tonight. I am at peace.

The ancient stones haunt me, the ancient stones of the poor. Many graves now lie unmarked and unremarkable here in the autumn dusk. Why did these people walk this way? Why did they come and die? To brighten the earth with a cheery smile? To hold a wee babe's wobbly head? The women of Little Bethel call me back and back. Back to a time when hardship and hard work were a way of life. Back to a time of thankless labor and early death.

Tell me, Little Sister's, I will relay your stories for you. The pen flies swiftly across the page, bringing your earth-locked message to the world. We will write of joy and sadness, we will write of birth and death, we will write of wisdom and knowledge, we will open the graveheld secrets and scatter them to the winds. Awake, Little Sisters, and tell me of the days so long ago, the days of yore, when you were wont to cry. Speak, Little Sisters, tell your tales of misery and woe. Free yourselves of the earthly shackles. Free yourselves to go. Shine Little Sisters, out from the dust. Speak, free yourselves at last. I wait to hear your call. I wait to tell your tale. Awake, Little Sisters. Awake. Speak, and find your place in the eternal round.

THE LITTLE SISTERS SPEAK

The ancients knew this spot. The Indians came later, recognizing the spot for its power and energy. The energy of the earth flows near the surface in this spot. The mining nearby and the gas wells have interrupted the natural flow of energy. Surgery on the earth disrupts the flow of energy just as surgery on the human body interrupts the normal flow. Never again is the exact proper balance achieved. The body, as well as the earth, heals itself the best way possible, but the desired balance and harmony are gone.

This area was and is still powerful because the power was so strong and near the surface. The ancients knew this and used the spot for worship. The Indians recognized the signs and used the area for the same purpose. Death and burial in this area have weakened the strength of the flow somewhat. The prayers that accompanied the departed reestablished the balance. Mining and rape of the land draw off energy which is not replenished. Burial draws off energy, but the prayers balance the load. For that reason burial in the earth is acceptable. Burial without prayer drains the earth because of the sadness that is unrequited by prayer. Loneliness returned to the earth remains. Fear and hatred remain. Love balances.

Many children died of fear and neglect. The families were so large that only those with strong inner strength survived the rigors of living. The strong souls withstood the many illnesses and hardships resulting from poor hygiene and improper diet. Hard work and a joyless existence destroyed those of a higher nature. Religion was strict and forbidding. Freedom of any sort was at a premium in this area. The cold winters and short summers meant hardship and toil for those who were able.

The young women, locked into motherhood too young and too often, were unable to withstand the demands placed upon them by the husbands who required a submissive wife. Little of joy remained in their lives as they laid their babies to rest and felt the unpleasantness of repeated deaths. Husbands demanded more than they were able to give, returning little in the way of support and love.

The hardy and hard survived. Many of the fairer, the spiritual, those who sought on a higher plane, could not withstand the cruelty of the lifestyle. Men were supreme in their own homes, the women were handmaidens, the weaker sex, to be exploited and used. Men demanded, the women submitted as the Bible was interpreted to them. Many could not give up self, could not tolerate the debasement and depersonalization. Hard work and a big family marked the sign of a worthy and honored woman. Never mind that she could not grow in her own way to become her own self. She was chattel to be used and abused. She was of little value. Needy but unneeded. There were more where she came from! The honored woman was the one who gave and gave until there was nothing left to give. She had given herself all away and could give no more.The grave received the shell of a spent and desperate soul. Life was hard and death was welcome. A relief from the rigors and demands.

We all welcome you to listen to us. We have waited so long for someone to hear the sad, sad story of the little daughters. The little daughters who sought so hard and tried for so long to reach the Master's table, only to be pushed aside by the multitudes who had died the martyrs death. Have we died in vain? Is there no one who will tell our story? Will you? Will you risk telling our story? Yes.

We are all around you here in this partially abandoned graveyard where so many of us came to rest and to lay our loved ones down. Our children cried and died never knowing happiness

6

or joy. Life was joyless. The work was hard. We tried so hard but there was never enough. Many of us died of malnutrition. There was not enough food for us and the little ones. There was never enough warmth, either physical or spiritual. Many of the stones that marked our passing have been discarded on the refuse heap. So were we! The bodies were not strong enough to withstand the demands placed by a stern and demanding lifestyle. Spiritual and emotional support was lacking. We could not give enough. The balance was not there. We are the ones who lost. We did not have time to achieve our destinies in that time and place.

We welcome you and cheer for you. Where have you been? Little sister, we have waited so long. We have needed you so badly. Tell our story to the world. Learn by it. Profit by it. Write in prose. Write as fiction if necessary, but tell our story of hardship, of pain, of toil and tears. Come to this spot and rest with us. There are many of us here. We have been waiting for so long! You will help us free ourselves of the burden of tears. The tears lie heavy on the ground. The air is full of tears, shed and unshed. The tears of generations of poor, hurting, unheard women. Be our mouth, be our ears, be our eyes. Tell our story to the world. Free us of torment. Prevent it happening to others. Help us to change the tide. Turn the page of history. Don't let the agonies of bygone days happen again and again. Seek us as we have sought you. Tell our story. The story of pain. The veil of tears, the veil of sighs, the veil of broken hearts. Laid to rest before our time because of the pain of brokenness and separation from our source of life and joy. Light fled from our lives with the pain. Light burned away in the cold and darkness. Rekindle the light. Help us find peace. Tell it as we tell you.

Come back. Take a rock with you. Feel our presence in that rock. Feel our sadness. Release it for us. We need you.

Night Message

Saturday, September 21, 4:30 AM.

We need you. You may sleep when we have given you more of our message. You will not be used up nor worn out. We need you too badly to wear you out. We are here in legion waiting to give you our message. All the little sisters have heard your call. We are many. We watched you through your struggle with the college and wanted to give you comfort. You have felt our pain and experienced our heartache. The story must be told. The cycle must be broken. We have suffered long enough. The soul of woman is sweet and simple. We bring peace to the world. Men bring discordance and disharmony as they blunder through,

7

pillaging and raping the land and her people.

Because you have suffered with us we give you our message. You are our spokesman now. You must speak the message, write the message, make the world hear.

NAHANA

My name is Nahana. I lived many years ago. The land was younger then. The seas covered more of the earth than they do now. We were a mighty race of white people. Our roots lay far away in a distant place and time. Hardship had come to us because the men of the world were in battle. They battled for power and from greed. We fled from the coast into the hills to avoid the great battle. The mountains were steep and rugged as we crossed. There was no room to rest. The winds were strong and cold and there were many wild animals who preyed on us. As we passed we followed the paths of the ancients who had passed this way before. They had left a well marked trail that we had no trouble in following although many of the rocks had tipped and fallen and much growth had occurred in the underbrush and trees. There were many obstacles blocking the way. When we arrived the village was in disarray and much destruction had occurred in the external edifices. We had little time to prepare ourselves for the winter, so we lost many people that winter to cold and disease. The land was inhospitable to those of us who survived. The cold ate into our very beings and in many destroyed the will to survive. Many of the children were lost and all the old people. There was no food for many months. We lived on roots and bark from trees. It was hard to gather our meager supplies because of the cold and our own weakness. We fought the cold with our great fires and drove the wild beasts back with shouting and fire sticks. Toward spring when our defenses were weakest, we were overtaken by a mighty army that destroyed what little hope we had for survival. They swept through our village killing and raping. They battered the few remaining children and drove all that were left into the wilderness to the north. Life was even worse than where we had been because of the ruggedness of the mountains and the cold.

Again, we followed the paths of the ancients hoping to find comfort. It had been too long! The external edifices were gone and the openings to the treasures and caves concealed. Only a few knew where to look and could not find the openings to the only place where we could find shelter from the storms and from the armies that drove us onward. They were mighty, strong, and cruel. They would not give us rest. They wanted our secrets and all our lives. We fled before them ever northward into the cold

8

and inhospitable land with no boundaries. The land from which no man returns. The land of eternal winter, ice and snow. Our meager supplies exhausted, we lay together on the ground, the winds howling, the snow blowing across us, and sought eternal rest. As our bodies froze, locked into an icy embrace, our souls departed. There were only a few of us left. The remnant of a great and mighty people, proud and free. We were peaceful and did not know how to fight. We had no weapons nor means of defense. Our only defense was to flee before the enemy who we did not see as enemy. We loved all people and sought peace on the earth. It was not to be then and has not been since.

The earth now holds our secrets as we buried our treasures along the way. Treasures of wisdom and knowledge that had been handed down to us from the ancients who had come from the far distant planet so long ago. The memories fade with time. The keys are lost. The language changes. People forgot how to read the messages of the ancients and the codes were lost. We had the treasures, but the keys to decipher were lost. We had lost our skills at telepathy. It was only a distant and indistinct memory.

Those who chased us and destroyed us thought we carried secrets that would make them rich and immortal. They were unable to see that we too died and struggled for existence. Their greed blinded them to truth. Their corruption shut them away from seeing and hearing the truth that lay before them. We had no secrets of immortality nor did we have riches to gain power. We had only the locked up secrets of the ancients and our will to survive. We desired to return to the peaceful life and would have reconciled with the chasers. They were too mighty, and they would not listen. We were allowed no negotiation. We would have given all to return to our homeland. Our homeland was destroyed and the peoples scattered to the ends of the earth. Many of us died. Only a remnant remained. They were so weakened that the little knowledge they did retain of the ancients was lost. Lost in the fogs and mists of the past. Memory dimmed, and the original dream was lost. The dream of a mighty nation beside a mighty sea. A nation based on love and peace, everyone living in harmony and perfect accord. Greed and jealousy were the downfall of that mighty nation by the sea. Greed of a few living in our own midst. The greed spread like a cancer until many were governed by it, giving their very lives to acquire more and more wealth. They became ruthless and cruel as they robbed and pillaged what others had to live with. There was plenty for all but those of the greed were not satisfied to have what the others had. They wanted more and wanted to be respected for what they had rather than for their demonstrations of love and caring. As the numbers of greedy increased those who would not fight to protect what they had were forced to flee before the attackers.

We tried to preserve the treasures of the ancients because of the messages therein but were unable to do so. We were unable to save them and unable to use them for survival so hid them.

Since the temples and edifices had fallen we were unable to find the shelter we had expected on the route. We were sorely disappointed at that. We had expected to find welcome and hospitality but the land was bare. (Nahana, you are not making sense. Are you making this up or am I?)

It does make sense! The land of the mountains was settled in the ancient times by the Fathers from the far distant planet. Some of the sons of the Fathers stayed by the seaside and some of the sons went into the mountains. Do you not do this now? Families do not stay together. Each has different tastes. The treasures were scattered as the sons moved about and settled into mighty communities. They shared together and prospered because of the sharing. It was not until the greed of a few became the greed of many that trouble became a way of life and we fled the danger. You are screening this through your understanding. Just listen and write. It will all make sense. You are learning the history of a mighty people, descendants of the Fathers who came from the far distant planets.

AMI

My name is Ami. I was only 4 summers old when I passed back through the veil of tears. I never could understand why life was so joyless. All about on every side stood glorious mountain peaks, giant oaks, maples, and the mighty evergreens. Water in mountain creeks plunged crystal clear down the mountain sides. Rocks abounded on every side adding a granduer to the landscape. Animals, too, were plentiful and had not yet learned the fear of man. White man had not yet penetrated our mountain stronghold. To the east and south he was being destroyed by white men, but we were safe so far. We lived in daily dread that white men would find the paths of the ancients breaching our mountain stronghold.

Our teepees were strong against wind and safe protection against cold. We spent little time in them though because the great outside was so much better.

My dog, Blue Feather, was my favorite friend. He went everywhere with me, showing me the fox's den and the rabbits lair. He was the prettiest dog in camp with his yellow eyes and yellowbrown fur. The day he was found the old chief wanted to drive him from the camp because he was so small and weak. Kindness softened the heart of the old chief when he saw that I too needed a friend. Blue Feather and I couldn't run fast like the other children in camp because we each came into this world with a twisted leg. The others would run from us and call us bad medicine. Blue Feather wasn't bad medicine any more than the Blue Jay feather I named him for and which he wore in the collar I made for him with strips of deer hide. It made Blue Feather look very pretty. I didn't feel like bad medicine. I don't think anyone could get a bad leg from me. I wasn't sick. I was born that way. Somehow, though, there was something bad wrong with me that I didn't know about, because even my parents didn't really want me around the camp. They gave me enough to eat to stay alive, but not enough to grow on and feel well. Once in a while Mama would slip me an extra piece of juicy meat from the cooking pot, but only when no one else was watching. She told me that there wasn't any use in growing up because none of the young braves would want me for wife anyway.

Papa wouldn't even look my way. It seemed that I was a poor reflection on his manhood. He was less brave because of my weak, crooked leg. How can that be? How can my leg make him weak? I am the one who falls and trips, who can't run with the others, and who gets teased and ridiculed. I don't know how that hurts him or Mama.

While the others play and do their work I help Mama clean the cooking vessels and clean the ground around the teepee. If we leave food droppings on the ground the animals from the forests come in to eat and might come in the teepee to get warm. The grownups all worry about that. I don't because the animals don't want to come in with us. Men smell too bad, so animals don't like our smell.

One day by the creek an otter showed me how he washed his food and told me where to find the best roots and the tenderest twigs. That helps with the hunger when there isn't enough food in the pot to go around, and I don't get any. Raccoons, too, tell me how to find food and how to swim. Blue Feather tells me how to stay away from the other children and hide from the taunts and jeers. He takes me deep into the woods where the trees grow close together and the rocks are high. We sit in our secret place and talk of the wonders of nature. He knows so much about how to use his nose to find a trail and how to track where the braves have passed. He knows the smell of a bear from that of a panther and teaches me the difference.

Blue Feather is my best friend. He knows all sorts of things that I need to know.

Winters in the high country are cold and raw. Winds howling about at night sound like the wild animals the elders talk about at the campfires. They tell strange stories of wild men and wild animals that have never been tamed. The wild men of the mountains they call them. There is fear in their voices when they speak of the wild men and animals. I've never seen one of these

11

strange creatures, but I don't want one in the teepee either.

We move into the valleys in the winter where the wind is not so strong and water is easier to find. Still, it is cold, and the snow grows deep. It is hard to walk in the snow with a weak leg. Blue Feather stays with me when I fall and makes sure that I don't stay there and freeze. Sometimes I have to hold his shaggy hair and let him help me to my feet. He is patient with me and doesn't growl when I pull his hair. He knows I don't mean to hurt him. He tells me where and how to hold so that he can pull better and it won't hurt him. Blue Feather is my very best friend.

One day I saw a flock of geese flying overhead. I wish that I could fly like that. I would like to be able to soar with the eagle over the mountain tops and away to a warmer place. They say at the campfires that there are places where the sun shines all year and there is never ice and snow. Blue Feather and I would like to go there to stay. Away from the cold and ice. Do you suppose the people there would be warm like the sun? Or would they too run from me or tease because of my different leg? It's hard to be different from everyone else. They don't seem to understand that I'm not different inside. I love and hate, I cry and laugh just the same as they do. What makes them think I am different inside because my leg is different on the outside? I don't understand it. How could I make trouble for people I don't even know? I don't make trouble for people I do know. I stay in the shadows and listen to what they say. They don't know I am there. That's how I know about the land of the eternal sun. When they don't see me or know that I am there I am safe. Blue Feather and I know how to stay in the shadows and never make a sound. We learn a lot that way.

Someday I want to go to the land of eternal sun and never feel the cold of the gray winters again. Oh, I like to see the snow on the pines and rocks. I will miss that. I like to see the snow crowned trees standing starkly against the sky. It is the cold that makes me hurt. The cold of the body and my crooked leg, but worse, the cold of loneliness. That empty cold core inside which never feels the warmth of love. Maybe it will be warmed in the land of eternal sun.

Blue Feather is my very best friend. He will go with me and help me find the way. He knows so much that I don't know. We will find the way together. When we find that land we will stay, never to return to the mountains again. I will miss the mountains and my valley home, but I will not pine the cold.

LETITIA

I am Letitia. I did not live many years. They called me

12

Lettie but I preferred Letitia. Lettie sounded like the name for a little girl. When you are fifteen you don't like to feel and sound like a little girl.

I well remember the winter that I died. The weather had been cold and damp all fall and the winter bore the same type cold and chill. I was having trouble breathing and found the fire in the cabin especially noisome that winter. Each time that Pa and the boys went outside a blast of smoke would fill the room making me cough and choke. The day the blood came, I knew that I did not have long to live. The scarlet on the white muslin was stark reality. I could no longer deny that my lungs were sorely diseased. For two years I had felt the increasing ravages of the diseases. Grandma and the twins had already died and were lying in the graves on the hill. I knew now that I too would soon join them in the ground. I did not look forward to the cold and dampness of the ground.

A traveling preacher came to the church last Sunday and told us that if we are not good we will burn in hell. He thought to scare us into being good. I have not had time to test life or taste its riches and splendor. Life has been cold and miserable. The fires of hell sound almost like a welcome change from the snow and cold!

There has always been so much to do since Ma died and left the twins just babies. They, with the others, were too much to care for. Ma died a borning the twins, John Mark and Paul Phillip, when I was thirteen. Grandma came to help out but she was old and sickly so was more trouble than help. Pa has been especially hard to please since Ma died. He expects everything to be done just as Ma did and without complaint. I grow bone weary. There is no time to play, to sing, to think. It is all hard work. The pain in my shoulders and hands grows almost unbearable as I carry the water from the spring at the bottom of the hill to wash the clothes, scrub the cabin, and cook the meals.

The twins, sickly at first because there was so little to eat, grew into active, nosey little boys. They added to my chores as they tore things and threw things around the cabin. I did not have the energy or strength to give them. The day they died Pa carried them outside in the rain and buried them in the little pine box he had made. They entered this life together, they played together, they suffered together, and died together. They will share eternity in the little pine box in the cold, damp, dark ground, never again able to run and play and sing their wordless tunes.

Why does death take the young ones? Why didn't they have a chance to live? Why is life so harsh? Since I was the oldest I saw Ma grow old and weary as each year she borned a new baby and laid it to rest on the hill. Only I and the twins survived our first year. The twins were only past their second birthday when the grim reaper took the toll and I not yet sixteen. I never learned to read a book. I never learned what lies on the other side of the mountain. People passing through tell us there are great things to see. A body of water that stretches farther than you can see and sailing vessels to cross the water and see people in other countries. People with brown, brown skin, yellow people with slanty eyes. I can't imagine even in my wildest imaginings what they would look like.

The only people I see are Pa and the people at church. The traveling preachers make me want to leave this place and look for myself. Maybe someday I will be able to see for myself. Pa and the other men go over the mountains for supplies and to sell wood and hides. They see the land beyond the mountains but they tell me I can't go because I'm a girl and girls has to stay home and keep the house and cook the meals. Somebody has to take care of Ma and the others who come by. An empty cabin does not last long. There are people moving in from the East daily and they look for empty cabins. They pass by if they see smoke at the chimney, unless they is hungry and then they stops to eat-share a bite they says! They don't share a bite becuz they doesn't bring a bite with 'um. They shares our bite and goes on! They takes the bite that should a bin mine or Ma's but hain't.

Pa sez that I cain't complain and grow rankled becuz he's a doin' the best he can. It sure is hard not to complain when the winter is so cold and I cain't get outside and see the sky. The smoke smarts our eyes and hurts our breathin'. How can a body be pleasant and joyous like the preacher sez if we are hungry and cain't breathe? I am always so tired! Too much to do, not enough time to do it. Hungry all the time and no one to talk to. God ain't close enough and I cain't see him, or touch him. He don't walk in here and ask, "What 'cha doin'?" He just 'posed to know I guess.

I miss Ma. When she felt like it, we would talk. She told me about God and how he loves us all. The preacher makes it look like God just sits there waiting for me to make one little slip so's he can slap me 'long side the head and send me right off to hell. I really get's confused 'cause Ma, she sez that God loves us, but I cain't see no signs of that. Why don't he warm the cabin and put food on the table if he loves us so good? Why does he keep takin' Ma's babies if he loves her so much? I jus' cain't understand that at all!

And yet, I don't understand what the preacher man sez. He sez that God punishes us for our sins and iniquities. Pa, he yells at me and hits me most every day 'cause I don't do things like he likes. If God punishes like Pa and the preacher sez, why don't he smite me dead and send me straight to hell? Life ain't all that great, but then hell don't sound that great either with all them sinners a weepin' and a wailin' and a gnashin' their teeth.

14

Maybe yet, that's why we don't have enough to eat. Maybe that's why the roof leaks and makes my bed wet which makes my cough worse. Maybe God is giving me my punishment for not doing what Pa wants and for not being a good girl. It is just too confusing! Why don't they make up their minds what they think God is, 'fore they starts telling me I don't know what to make of nothin' since Ma died.

I'd sure like to know what is so all fired great about this life that we is supposed to treasure. Pain, hunger, suffering, death. Is that beauty, joy, and peace? I think not!

ANNIE

I am Annie. It is hard to reach you through the veil of tears. The veil of tears is heavy and cold. So much sadness has collected about the world that it is hard to penetrate to the veil of joy. We have waited for one to speak for us. The men have spoken often but the women are neglected in death just as they were in life. We waited and yearned for someone to speak for us. Finally you are here. We will try not to wear you out, but all of us want to speak. The others are pushing on me and urging me to give you my story before they do and before I pass onward. This side is more complicated than those of you on that side realize. I am nearing a point where I will be elevated to a higher plane which makes it harder to contact those of you on earth.

No, I will not give you my whole name. It is not necessary to trace and confirm who we are. It is unnecessary. You must believe. It would cause too much heartache if you would announce who we are. The temptation would be there to share with the families. That must not be. You are not to do seances and charlatan type things. You must not use this to gain profit or fortune on the misery of others. You are to publish and spread the message-not reap sensationalism. Do what we have asked. Don't become a charlatan. The temptation is always there and great. Resist it. You will profit without having to desecrate the graves and prostitute your own wisdom. Be patient.

I am Annie. I lived in the valley beneath the towering hills. The mountains were our protection against storm and winds. Life was harsh when I lived. We had a one room cabin cut and hewn by Caleb and the boys. There were five boys living and able to help with the work and chores. The work for the men was hard because of the wild beasts and the cold and snow in the winter. The beasts would get hungry and come to the farm for food. We never had any to spare for wild beasts. Many winters there was not enough food for us to feel comfortable. We could not share with the wild beasts.

15

Sometimes bears would get into the stores and ruin most of what we had laid away for winter. They were real mean about killing the fatted hogs. They waste more than they eat. It makes a body sad to see waste and know that the least ones will be hungry all winter and may not live to see the spring.

Death in the winter is a sad and troublesome thing. We watch the wasting away and feel the hopelessness. Too many times death comes silently in the night when the wind is creaking the roof shingles and we can't hear the breathing of the little ones in the loft. Come morning, there's a cold, lifeless body among the warm live ones. The sadness is almost unbearable. How many times must we born the children only to watch them die before they have the joys and pleasures of life?

In the winter the preaching man only gets here when the trails and roads are passable. Too often death comes when the preachin' man don't. We either have to keep the body or put it in the ground without blessin'. Keepin' the body is hard to do. Animals smell the death and come to peer and then sometimes to ravage the body. A wee corpse ravaged by a savage bear is not a pretty sight for anyone's eyes, leastways the girls. They seem to cry and take on more than the boys. Not just about the ravagin' of the body, but, too, 'bout the death and the needs here in the hills. Maybe they have a sense of what is to be their lot in this pain filled, woeful world.

Try as we can, there is never enough warmth to chase the chill in the winter. The walls grow damp from the fires and us livin' there and the mud falls out of the chinkin'. Wind and cold air seep in around every door and finds holes that we don't know is there.

Time is long in the winter when the ground lies frozen and bare. 'Bout the only thing we hope for in the winter is the first thaw where the earth begins to awaken and we can shake the winter scales from our souls. The soul shrivels with the cold in the winter. Loneliness creeps in with the first fogs of autumn and lingers here until summer brings travelers to our door. The preachin' man comes again and we get together to see who lived through another cold, barren winter.

I enjoy getting out of the cabin and feeling the fresh, clean air. It is so refreshing after the smoke and damp of the cabin in the winter. We throw open the doors and take the boards and packing off the windows. The sun comes in and lights the room. Away the least ones go to the woods to look for nuts left from fall. Not many do they find. The squirrels make sure of that! I think the hardest part of spring is to see the little ones go to play and know that death has taken one away. No matter how many babies a body bears, the one who slipped away in the night is sorely missed. The wound of emptiness never quite heals as we try to go on without him. God, would that I would never have to lay another little one to rest!

The men have gone to the woods to cut some trees. We need to build a tighter barn this year. I worry about them in the woods. The trees are so big and close together that it is hard to get a clear fall. Too many men and boys are killed or hurt by branches and trees knocked over by the timber fall.

Down the road a piece lives old man Tom. Walks with a stick and cain't do much 'cause a tree hit his foot and leg. That once straight leg looks like a letter 'S' now and pains him terrible. Seems when that tree fell on him it not only broke his leg but broke his spirit as well. The whole bunch down there watches out when he get's het up-and it don't take much to het him up neither!

I remember one Sabbath Day when me and the kids was walkin' down past his house to go to meetin'. Why, for no good reason at all, he sicked that ornery cur dog of his'en on me and the kids. Seemed all he wanted to do was to see them kids run and scream. The girls, they didn't run. They was too skeered to move and just let that old cur dog go chase the boys. That old man Tom just sat there on his stool in the shade and laughed fit to kill. Don't know why some people take such pleasure in seeing another hurt or skeered. The preaching man, he sez we all have to love each other or we will go to hell. Now, I cain't figure this out. Why do I have to love old man Tom when he don't love me and my kids? Don't you think it is just a wee bit hard to love someone who does mean things to you and your kids? I ponder this often and yet it wonders me how anyone can love a man as ornery as old man Tom.

I weep now for my little ones and wonder why they were taken. How did they anger the God of Wrath? What kind of orneriness could they a done to have God snatch them away like that? That's another thing that wonders me. Why does God punish the little ones and take them away from life when they ain't done nothin' and leave old Tom down there, cussin' and ornery, to sic that cur dog on innocent children just trying to get to meetin'?

There is just too much to figure out! Is life a punishment? Is this the cross we bear? It sure don't seem like heaven the way we bear these younguns and put them in the ground, the way the innocent get took and the ornery stays.

Leastways, I know the veil of tears is rent every time a little one passes and he goes on to be with God. Mayhap he is better off than the rest of us on this side of the veil, 'cause he don't never have to feel the cold and wind in the dark, damp winter cabin. He don't never have to feel the hunger no more, the hunger of the body for food and the spirit for comfort. He don't have to ponder the great wonderments. He rests peacefully beyond the veil of tears. I too will step beyond the veil and see

17

my least ones face to face. My empty arms will cradle them and feel the fulness that was stolen away in the night. Death holds no fear. The cold and lonely winter is worse.

LONEY

Age: 1 Year, 10 Months, 13 Days

My name is Loney. I am one of the least ones. The older ones push me away when I come to the veil of tears. They think their message is more important than mine. I, too, suffered through the cold, damp winters and felt the chill of the wind. I, too, felt the loneliness and fear of a stark, mountain existence.

I died in the summer when the days were hot and dry. The sun was hot, and a hot wind blew across the land. The laurels and rhododendrons drooped and curled their leaves. The creeks ran dry, and we did not have water in the spring. Pa would walk back into the mountains to find water where it ran out of the rocks. Everyone for miles around used the same water along with the animals.

As the hot weather continued the water became tainted with mud and the offal of the animals who came to drink. Try as he might, Pa always scooped up some of the droppings with the water. Many who drank of the water died that summer. They called it summer complaint.

What I remember of that hot, dry summer was the thirst, always the thirst. The body grew feverish with the thirst, and then the bowels began to gripe. Not just once a day or twice a day but many times a day. As the amount increased, the need for water grew worse. We were all thirsty for pure, clean water without any filth. That was not to be found.

As the summer dragged on and the thirst and diarrhea increased, I could feel my body withering away. Ma was not able to feed me at her breast because of her weakness and thirst. The food they gave me was too coarse and did not agree with me. Always I had hunger, thirst, and a hurting in my stomach. I could feel my lips cracking and sore from the dryness and my eyes sinking into my head. My vision blurred as the weakness grew.

The day I left I didn't really want to go. Ma was crying and the bigger children watched in wonderment as I tried to breathe and find some moisture for my lips. I heard them say, "Loney is almost gone. She's so weak and her bowels are bleeding." I wasn't sure what they meant but I knew that I was too weak to do more than whimper in pain. The swelling in my belly was painful, only adding to the torture.

LONEY'S SONG OF DEATH

Too soon this life is ending.
Too soon the veil is rent.
Too soon I leave the valley
Where my short life was spent.

Too fast the days went fleeting
From birth until death.
Too fast the shadows darkened
And stopped my heart from beating.

Farewell to all the days
That were to mark my life.
Farewell to things undone, unsaid.
Farewell, farewell I'll never be a wife.

Too soon the shadows lengthen,
Too fast the minutes fleet,
Farewell to all the family,
I had never chance to strengthen.

I will miss the joys of singing,
I will miss the robins song.
I will miss the gushing
water sound down the hills ringing.

Farewell to Bob and Angeline,
Farewell to Dick and Rose.
Farewell to Ma and Papa too.
I will miss your . . .

The sounds of the earth are like music to my ears.
The sights of the earth are a deep, deep pleasure.
Why do I yearn to stay
When painful has been my way?

I did not learn the mysteries
Of the twinkling stars at night.
Of the moon and sun
And what makes the wild deer run.

I've not had time to learn of love and honor,
Of pleasure and of gain.
I've only felt the fleeting moments of life
And then, the stillness of the grave.

Why was life so short and sad?
Is that what life is for?
To teach a young soul sadness,
To wipe the joy away?

Will I ever know the joy of time?
Will I ever feel the rain?
Life's fleeting moments
Spent alone and in pain.

Where was the love that softens pain?
Where was the tender kiss?
No one knew how the little one sorrowed
And cried for the tender caress.

I flee away beyond the veil
To loftier sights and sounds,
To float away in misted bliss
To the place where love exists.

Lay me low in the cold, dark ground
And raise my monument high.
Future children will read my name
And shed a tear of sadness for the wee, small babe
Who's dying breath whispered one small word,

WHY?

LONEY SPEAKS AGAIN

Yes, I want to speak to you again. As I told you before I was one of the least ones. Life was short and painful. I was born in the fall when the leaves were falling from the trees. The struggle to enter was difficult. Ma was so weak and tired from all the other bornings, hard work, and poor food that she just didn't have the strength to help me leave her body. She knew when I got there it would be another mouth to feed and more chores. I knew I would be a burden to her and crowd an already crowded existence.

The battle through the veil of tears was even harder. Ma didn't want another baby so the sadness was so great that my soul withered before I ever saw the light of day. Darkness and despair covered the hillside house and farm like a thick, suffocating blanket through which joy and blessing were unable to penetrate. A joyless existence on a joyless trek through a joyless lifetime.

So much energy and time was wasted in the despair and gloom of that miserly existence No one saw the beauty of the fall colors abounding all around. No one cared that the wild goose passed overhead honking his way south to a warmer clime and time. The wild goose didn't stop at our hill home because he too felt the drab and cheerlessness that permeated the air and very soil of the place. Mighty rocks rose all around, but the despair-locked mortals groveling along the paths, couldn't raise their eyes or raise their souls to absorb the power and strength the rocks offered in such abundance. Rather, they walked always with downcast eyes, cursing the rocks, for impeding their progress.

Loney's Song of Why

O mortal man, how foolish are you in your ways.
You curse the ground that gives you strength
And walk about with downcast eyes,
Failing to see the splendors around you.

Failing to look up with hope and pride,
Failing to seek the God
Who gave you life and offers
Abundance for the asking.
You fail to see the myriad stars
Shining against an ebon sky
And never stop to wonder why.
You curse the sun for too much heat,

21

Then curse the day that the sun doesn't shine.
You curse the heat and you curse the cold.
What makes man so foolish?
Why can he not see the beauty
In a caterpillars shiny skin?
Or feel the beauty
Of the bull frogs call?
Why does he not look deep into the center
Of the smallest flower
And see the Universe unfold?
Despair and gloom would sweep away
If only he would stop and say,
"What a beautiful day,
What a beautiful life,
What a beautiful world
You have given us."
Instead he fears the dark and unknown,
Locking himself into the citadel
Of his own rock bound existence.
He hardens himself to the beauties
And the wonders lying all about,
Surrounding him on all sides
And towering o'er his head.
Why can he not look up and say,
"God, I am one of your small ones.
Show me the way."
Why can he not then trust this God
Who promises to give us all?
Why can he not feel the love
And share the peace and calm
That are there for all?

I don't understand why the little ones were never given say. We knew the wonders of the universe, but only the elders were considered wise. Where is the wisdom in downcast eye? They may not stumble on a pebble but they surely will walk into the stone wall. Better to risk a small trip over a pebble than to miss seeing the wonders all around, above and below.

Life was short and not too dear. Death came as a welcome from the pain, despair, loneliness, and sadness of that poor hill family. Could they but see what I saw in my short sojourn there, they could never again cast the downward eye, but would go into eternity looking upward and onward. Peering into the smallest crevice, seeking the woolly spider, seeking along the mountain paths for the beauties unsurpassed, ever casting the eye skyward to seek the great "out there." What a difference it would make, if only they would seek the beauty, forgive the wrong, and live

in harmony with the elements.
The existence there was harsh and cruel. I could see the future and what was in store for me. The veil of tears hung all about, closing me in and shutting away the joy. It was not a hard decision to step through the veil and leave the earthly existence behind. O they mourned a little bit. But already a new babe was on the way. My replacement, if you may. From beyond the veil of tears I look back with no regrets that my stay on earth was so short. Never have I sought a return to the joyless existence I found there. God, in his infinite wisdom, sent me for a short time to taste the pain and sorrow, then removed me to a higher plane to rest throughout the ages.

The Never Ending Question

Time without dimension,
Time without time,
An infinity of beingness,
An ocean of mild endeavor.

The beginning and the end,
The circle without end.
Ever in tune with the
Greater scheme of things.

Afloat in the vastness.
Still my whispered question
Lies within my heart.
The never ending question.

The question without answer.
The question?
WHY?

BECKY

My name is Becky. Rebecca to the big folks. That was the name they gave me at birth. Don't know why they puts a name to ya' and then calls ya' somethin' else. Anyway, that's what they done. Named me Rebecca Eleanor and then they called me Becky. Now they don't seem to realize how confusing that is. Who am I? Rebecca, Rebecca Eleanor, or Becky? Are we all the same? Or are we three different ones? Is there a Rebecca inside the Becky and a Becky inside the Rebecca Eleanor?
When Ma gets mad she yells Rebecca Eleanor so I most has it figured out that Rebecca Eleanor lies somewhere inside of Becky

and is a bad, bad girl. She makes me do the things I don't want to do and gits me in trouble. She's the one who poured the milk on the cabin floor to see the pattern it would make on the rough boards. She pushed the gate open to let the chickens roam, then followed them to the woods to see where they would go and what they does there in the cool shadows below the mighty trees.

Rebecca Eleanor hates to go to meeting when the preachin' man comes. She gits so tired of sittin' on the hard, hard boards. Her legs hurts as they hangs in the air and the board on her back is a terrible pain! The preachin' man screams, "Repent, Repent, and mend your ways." He talks straight to Rebecca Eleanor but she don't listen 'cause she's alookin' out the window at the birds in the maple by the gate. She sees the flies a walkin' on old farmer Burner's bald, bald head. Why, do you know that fly just walked all over, up and down, back and forth, just like farmer Burner does when he plows his field? It stepped over them scraggly hairs just like he does when he carries the rocks to the heap in the corner of the field. That fly never once fell offen that smooth head, even when he had to lift his legs high to step over a log of hairs.

Rebecca Eleanor cain't go to sleep in church 'cause that's ag'in the rules. Ma, she don't 'low sleepin' and neither do the elders. Who could sleep anyhow, no matter how tired they is, with that preacher man up there a screamin' and a hollerin' in the name of God. I can't figure it out. Why does he need to scream and shout about the way to get to heaven when the whole thing is just plain simple! Rebecca Eleanor knows that all she has to do is ask God to hold her hand and help her not to stumble.

Rebecca Eleanor counts every bench in that ugly, stark, church and knows the tombstones outside her window. When she gets home she goes to her secret place and ponders 'bout the ones who have gone before. What did they do and where did they go? Did they like to sit in the hard, hard pew any better than she does? What happened to the little ones? Did they die abornin'? Did their souls have time to flourish? Was their Ma good to them? Did they feel the cold and damp of winter? Did they ever feel the warm, gentle rain on their faces? Did they ever hear the hoot owl callin' through the night or cry with the dove as it sings its' mournin' song? Rebecca Eleanor asks many, many questions.

She is never still and never quiet. She seeks and searches and loves a good time. Too bad Rebecca Eleanor can't be on the outside instead of always locked away on the inside. When she does get out the end is always the same! She gets Becky in trouble and Pa and Ma gets mad. Best to leave her locked away inside. I know she is there. And you know what? I don't think she's all that bad. Now Rebecca, on the other hand, is more the lady. She sits still in meeting cause she wants to please Ma and the elders. She walks primly on the way to meeting, not like

Rebecca Eleanor who wants to skip and run. Rebecca keeps her Sunday dress clean and wrinkle free. She sits carefully and daintily and never squirms. She never shouts or screams. Rebecca Eleanor, though! That's a different thing. She doesn't want to walk in dignity and sit with graceful poise. She chases the butterfly and falls in the creek. While watching a bird fly by a white, white cloud, she steps into a mud puddle and soils her shoes and stockings. While picking the wild blackberries, she snags her Sunday dress. Rebecca just can't keep Rebecca Eleanor under control!

Becky is the one who does the chores and comes when Ma calls. She washes dishes, scrubs the floor, and watches after the young 'uns. But all the time she knows down deep inside of her that Rebecca Eleanor and Rebecca are in a mighty fight. Rebecca Eleanor says, "Let's go out to play. The sun is bright and the flowers are abloom. Let's run into the woods and follow the path to the hills. Let's sit on a stump and gaze at a toad and search for the riddler's maze. Let's flee to the hill and soar through the skies on dreams and fairytale lies. Let's leave this drudgery and leave the toil. Let's seek where the wild flowers bloom. Watch a bee, wade a creek, lie on our back in the sun. Leave the house and leave the chores, leave the earth-binding ways. Flee to the hills and look to the sky, the reflection of God's great power."

Rebecca, down inside says, "No. The chores must be done. We want the dishes washed so clean and the cabin floors dirt free. Our mountain shack is not a shack, but a castle, proud and gleaming. We have the riches of the earth at our fingertips. The grand lady of a grand mansion. All the children clean and well mannered, gentlemen and ladies resting after the days labors."

Becky often runs and hides 'cause she gets so confused. Which girl is she really? The two who lie inside of her or the one called Becky who tries her best to keep it all in check? Becky loves to sing and dance, more like Rebecca Eleanor. She doesn't really like the meetin' house, but waits patiently for the last amen. Becky greets the neighbors with polite and pleasant refrain. She doesn't really mind the mess made by Rebecca Eleanor. Let Rebecca be upset! Becky knows that Rebecca Eleanor must be free.

When death came and the veil was rent, the name on the tombstone read, Rebecca Eleanor, Age 10 Years, 5 Months, 21 Days. Rebecca Eleanor, the deep, deep sister, freed from Rebecca and the hold of Becky. Little did the family know that Rebecca Eleanor was free at last. Free of the shackles of earthly ways and free to soar through the blue, blue skies. Soar like a bird and never fall, cross the creek without getting wet, examine a caterpillar and talk to a toad.

Rebecca Eleanor. Free at last!

REBECCA ELEANOR SPEAKS

The fall days in the hill country are beautiful and warm. I remember with fondness the days of going deep into the woods to gather nuts. We took oak split baskets and heaped them high with acorns, black walnuts, beech nuts, hickory nuts, and hazel nuts. We usually took a picnic and made a grand occasion of it. I especially liked this because on these days Becky would let the young'uns play and let Rebecca Eleanor out.

Ma, she was usually in a happy mood when we went to the woods and got away from the cabin and the chores. She would play with the little ones and show them how to make baskets out of burrs, necklaces out of Black Eyed Susan's, and how to catch a crawdad in the creek. We all had fun on those days. Ma's face would look different, younger and freer, somehow.

Sometimes I would wish that we could spend all our days in the cool, crisp fall air beneath the golden boughed trees and never have to go back to the closeness of the cabin. That could never be. 'Long toward evenin', when the shadows laid slantwise on the floor of the woods, we would pick up all our baskets and leave the smiles and laughter behind as we headed back to the cabin. As we drew nearer the cabin Ma's face would look tired and drawn, the look of ageless suffering would creep back in her eyes.

Not all was drudgery and work in that hill cabin, but the days of pure joy and freedom were few. Pa and the boys worked hard to clear the land and raise enough food to feed the hungry family. Seemed that wild animals were plentiful until the dead of winter when the real hunger set in and then they too was scarce. Pa set traps along the creeks and in all the right places, but, day after day, in the cold and snow, the traps were empty. Pa would return empty handed and hollow eyed, sorry to see the hunger growing and gnawing at us all.

Summer now. That was different! We all liked summer best. The woods were full of berries and fruits, free for the pickin'. Streams, broken free of the icy winter cover, were filled with fish and crawdads. Wild game was plentiful and fat. The little game we saw in the winter always looked gaunt and starved.

The summer sun was a welcome thing in the cabin. We could leave the doors open and enjoy the breeze and clean air. The young'uns could run out to play, so wasn't always under foot. Ma and I could finish the chores in the house and get out in the sun ourselves. It took a lot of sun to chase the winter chill out of our bones.

Spring was good because we knowed summer was right ahead. But the rains made the cabin damper than the winter and mud covered everything. Try as they might, everyone coming in that door brought mud and filth in on the floor. Our clothes got dirty and damp. They never seemed quite dry although we hung them in front of the fireplace to dry overnight. Spring was good though because the green shoots made good eatin'. A welcome relief from the poor winter fare.

One thing that I didn't like about spring was Ma's spring tonic. We all had to take it, from the oldest to the least one. I don't rightly know what all went into that tonic, but I do know, it tasted powerful bad! She would go into the woods and gather things and up under the eaves in the loft to bring down leaves from last years pickin'. She would crumble those leaves in a pot, stir in water from the spring and throw in the things gathered in the woods. After mixin' and stirrin' that vile brew over the fire until it looked just right, she would call us all in to the table and pass the potion 'round. Each received according to his size. That was one of the worst things 'bout growin' up. Each year there was a little more of the brew to drink. The little ones got a dash of honey in theirs', if there was honey left from last fall. But us older ones were admonished to take it as it came from the pot 'cause its better for you that way. It didn't do a bit of good to complain or go on 'bout it 'cause we had to drink it anyway. For days after the drinkin', ever time I thought of that vile poisonous taste the bile would rise into my throat and I would have to fight the need to run outside and heave that stuff into the grass. We all knew better than to do that though, 'cause if Ma heard that, she gave a second round from the store she saved for just such a purpose.

I remember one summer when the preachin' man come to the church house for a whole week. He come riding a horse over the mountains bringing his message of redemption to us poor mountain folks. Every night he stood up in that pulpit screaming and shouting, "Repent, repent, the day of the Lord is at hand. Repent, ye sinners, give up your foolish ways. Gold and silver corrupt, don't let gold and silver corrupt you. Give it to me and I will take it far away where you will not feel the corruption thereof. Now don't that just seem silly? We don't have all that much gold and silver here in the mountains anyhow. Most of the tradin' we do is for goods, not gold and silver. And I really have to wonder why gold and silver will corrupt us'in and not him. What a kind man he is to help us out and save us from burnin' in hell 'cause we has harbored gold and silver! All that week people from all over come in there and listened to that man yell in the name of the Lord. This jus' don't make sense to me. Why does he scream and shout? We can hear. We have ears. We ain't deaf. He screamed and ranted, then he said, "Let's all stand an' sing 103, Rock of Ages." Now if God is so deaf that we have to shout and scream to make him hear, then why would I want that rock to split so's I could hide myself in it? Wouldn't that be a

turrible thing to be a hidin' there in that rock with all that noise a bouncin' and a echoin' back and forth! I think I would ruther be out in the woods on the side of the hill a sittin' on top of that old rock a lookin' off to the mountains. I cain't see any reason why I'd like to hide myself down inside that cold, dark rock.
Can you?

THE VEIL EXPLAINED

Little Sisters, you speak of the veil of tears. What is the veil of tears?

We are the Little Sisters and we will gladly answer your question. We have all passed through the veil of tears both coming and going. You too have passed through it at various times, but did not recognize it for what it is.

The veil of tears lies like a pall over the earth. It surrounds the entire earth and is made up of all the sadness, pain, loneliness, tears, suffering, and heartache of all the people who have ever lived. In some areas the veil is very thick, heavy, and dense. In these areas it is extremely hard to penetrate. The worst areas lie over lands where people have been in constant battle and where there is great suffering.

You were in the veil in the vision in which you were singing and floating up and down among the bank of beings. These souls have been trapped there and are unable to free themselves until they work their way up and out of it. They are held in the pall by their own loneliness and hurt. You moved up and down through the veil and saw the differences. Toward the earth the veil is much thicker and heavier. The souls caught here have more earthly tendencies and more of the earthly characteristics. Their weight of hurts holds them down. As they are able to give up these hurts and the desires of the earth they move upward, losing the earthly accruements and acquiring more ethereal qualities. The soul becomes unweighted, so rises higher.

Some become aware of the veil as they are passing to the earth for birth into a physical existence. Loney was especially aware of that. Hers, as you noticed, is a very sensitive, poetic soul, easily hurt, and aware of many things. She did not have time in life to lose her awareness.

The veil or pall hangs heavily over areas of the earth where there has been much suffering. Africa today is adding heavily to the pall. Each child born into the misery and starvation enters with the weight of the veil pushing upon him. On death he then adds his misery and that of his mourning family to the pall. A heavy veil lies over all land areas where battles are going on and people are dying and suffering. Fear adds to the veil as do shed and unshed tears. The whole world is adding to the pall through

28

the threat of Nuclear War and the fears engendered by the threat.

The veil that Loney felt over her hill home was thick and heavy because of ancient sufferings that had occurred there. Indians too had suffered there and then the miseries of the impoverished family that she entered held the veil close to earth. The family was not only impoverished of the necessities of physical existence but were enormously impoverished of spiritual treasures. Loney could only survive a short time. Her beautiful spirit struggled, trying to bring some light and comfort into that pitiful home, until she could give no more. She would not have stayed as long as she did had she not had such pure love for the world. Her body was not strong and the living conditions certainly were not conducive to life.

You saw the band around the world. This is the major veil or pall. Locally, and closer to earth, there are smaller areas where the veil hangs close, rather like small veils lying over isolated areas. Loney's home, for instance, suffered under the larger veil, but also had a small veil surrounding it. This smaller veil consisted of the harsh, cruel lifestyle which the family lived. You might think of it as a cloud lying about the farm with the moisture of that cloud seeping into the buildings and the very land itself. The veil was so heavy there that Loney spoke of geese feeling it as they flew high overhead honking their way south to a warmer clime and time. She spoke also of having to battle through it as she entered physical life.

The veil of joy is the same thing created from the love and joys of life. The veils may exist simultaneously and in balance. It is when the veil of tears outweighs the veil of joy that people feel depression, hurt, hopelessness, and helplessness. The veil of joy is powerful and may be used to push away the veil of tears. Each time that a true prayer is uttered, the veil of joy grows thicker. Love and harmony add to the veil of joy.

You could see this as the opposites, good and evil, positive and negative feelings. It is the collected feelings that lie about an area, the totality. The negative feelings, or the veil of tears, can be dissipated by love and prayer. You helped to raise the veil of tears from your daughters house. The veil that had settled with the previous tenants. The veil of joy is not strong there because there has been little of joy in that house and on that ground. She and her family must make their own veil of joy in the house and around it.

You felt the veil over Little Bethel. The lifestyles and the land here were hard on the women, especially. The men suffered too, but not as much as the women. Men were better able to move about in the cold winters because their clothing was better suited to cold weather and snow. Skirts were cumbersome and uncomfortable as they collected moisture and mud.

The finer nature of women made them more vulnerable to

29

the confinement in houses during the winter months and to the lack of beauty in the lifestyle. Duties of the women kept them confined in the house while men worked outside in nature. Smoke and dust in the cabins contributed to much illness. Boredom too was a major contributing factor to poor health. There was plenty to do to maintain life, but the repetition and drudgery of it did not challenge the mind.

Spiritual starvation was prevalent. There were few books to read and little chance to discuss the nature of life and the Universe. Religious teaching was full of "thou shalts" and "thou shalt nots" with little thought given to the needs of the individual. Souls of poetic or sensitive nature languished in the starkness of the reality of the situation.

Isolation of families led to a solidification of thought patterns and religious expression, along with language idiosyncrasies. Patriarchal family systems kept the women's spirits' suppressed and confined within rigorous rules of deportment and conduct. Rebecca Eleanor especially felt this. Her true nature desired freedom of expression, but the teachings of home and church suppressed her true nature. The resultant confusion was more than she could bear.

DELIA

Welcome, my name is Cordelia. They didn't call me Cordelia, though. That was too much. They called me Delie. That's what they should have put on the grave marker because that's all I ever knew. I lived over by the blue mountains. It was a long way to come to meetin' but that's where God was. We passed many a church house on the way but Pa says that, "God ain't there. Those people trucks with worldly things and invites the devil to their table." Now, I don't want the devil or any of his kin at my table, so I guess Pa is right. Ma don't say nothin'. Pa says Ma and girls don't know nothin' nohow, so we don't argue with him. He has a way of makin' us agree anyhow, when he takes an apple switch to our legs. He says, "Hike them skirts." We hike 'em and he lays into our bare legs with that apple switch.

I remember one time he made blood run down Ma's legs 'cause she couldn't get up and fix his supper. She had summer complaint and just lost a baby a bornin'. He said, "There ain't no reason for a healthy, strong woman of his'n to lie around in bed lettin' the young'uns run." Ma looked so white and pale a lyin' there on the straw pallet, but Pa didn't keer. He said he'd been workin' in the woods all day and needed a bite to eat. He made Ma get up offen that bed of pain and sorrow, sick as she was, and fix him somethin' to eat. When he got finished he says to her, "Get up offen that bed, you lazy, good for nothin' daughter of Satan." When she got herself up, with no help from him, he tol' her to hike her skirts and he lit into her with a fireplace stick. Now Ma, too weak to run or holler, jus' stood there lettin' the tears run down her face and took that beatin'. Pa didn't stop until the floor was sprinkled with her blood. After that none of us kids ever tried to do nothin' to displease Pa. He had a quick hand with a switch or strap.

Seemed that the boys got some too, but there was always more beatin' for the girls. He'd say, "Boys will be boys." He'd never say, "Girls will be girls." I guess girls is just naturally supposed to be better than boys. It's hard sometimes to know what Pa wants. He says, "Delie, come here, Pa wants a kiss." But when I'd get up to his cheer he would smack me in the face or pull my hair, then laugh. He had the meanest laugh of anybody I've ever heard. Ma and us would listen for that laugh when he was a comin' home from the woods. You could hear it all over those mountains, bouncin' back and forth. He'd laugh at the strangest things. They never seemed funny to me. Seemed the more he could hurt a body and make them bleed, the more he would laugh. The same with animals. He nearly killed an old horse he had one time. He traded some ginseng to a peddlar from down east for an old, sway back horse. That horse knowed right from the start he was playin' a dangerous character in my old Pa. He tried his best to do what Pa wanted. He'd pull stumps all day or snake logs out of the woods, workin' and a sweatin' as if his life depended on it. It did! Ol' Pa, he would beat that old horse all day long to make it work harder, then when he came in for the evenin' he would give it half the ration and beat it agin', cause it didn't pull hard enough or it stumbled on a root.

Pa could cuss as good as he could laugh at other people's hurts. He'd pound and cuss that old horse somethin' terrible. Well, that old horse won over my old man. One day when Pa was a drivin' him in through a hot summer evenin', that old horse laid down, gave a sigh, and never got up agin'. Now, Pa didn't laugh that evenin'. No, sir! He was mad! Fit to be tied! That horse laid down right in the middle of the track and wouldn't budge until he was plumb dead. Pa had to drag that horse off into the woods and hide it so the wild animals wouldn't come sniffin' around after that dead meat. That kind of thing lying around a cabin yard can make a terrible smell and call in all kinds of dangerous beasts. When Pa got through buryin' that ol' horse he was a sweatin' and a gruntin' and just plain ornery mad. That night we was all quiet as could be so that Pa wouldn't see us. The older kids stayed in the woods that night. Us younger ones couldn't do that so we just stayed quiet and hoped Pa would forget we was there.

Ma tried to keep things neat around the cabin and give us enough to eat. What I liked best was in the summer when she would find time to pick some bright wild flowers and bring them in the house. Pa thought that was silly and sometimes he throwed them out. At night after Pa went to sleep I could hear Ma lyin' there cryin', quiet like. She didn't want Pa or us kids to hear her, so she would do it real quiet.

Many's the time that I thought that when I grew up and became a Ma, I would bring in flowers ever'time I could and I'd put them all over; on the mantle, on the table, on the cupboard. They make the cabin look so much prettier. I like pretty things. There ain't much of beauty in our cabin though. The beauty lies in the hills and trees, the flowers and the little wild animals.

Death was welcome in that rude hill house. Death came often in that crude hill house. Death was the only release. The only freedom. It was the only way to see my favorite little sister. She died so young we didn't get to know her well. I wait for her. She waits for me. We will be together someday.

Tell my story. Hold my candle high. My monument has gone to dust. Only my memory lies in the air.

Thank you for hearing and telling my story.

Sarah Elizabeth

I was born on a crystal spring day in 1861 in a hill cabin. I was the thirteenth babe born to the same Ma. She was spent and weary when I came along. She did not want me but had done her wifely duties and was giving birth for the thirteenth time. Not all the babes had lived. There were only a few in the cabin. I did not live long either. Just as I drew my first breath of air, I heard the death knell and passed back through the veil. It had been a hard struggle getting through the veil to reach that home and an equally hard struggle to return. Pain and suffering lay heavy on the hills around that rude log house. There had been many deaths and much suffering. My Mama was not an old woman, but her body was worn and tired. Before I was born she labored through the cold winter trying to find food for the young children in the home. Pa was gone. They talked of the war there in the cabin. "The dispute," they called it. There seemed to be disagreement over who should rule this vast country into which I was entering. Pa had gone North to find the Armies of the North. His brother, Lem, had gone South to find the Southern fighting men. Ma didn't want either one to go. She was afraid that they would not be able to come home. She feared that death would overtake them while they were away.

Their absence made it hard on Mama since it was up to her to keep the animals away from the livestock, keep the house warm and feed all the children. Little help did she have. I could feel the weakness mounting in her body as the time for my birth approached. Many days she was hungry and tired and unable to give me the nourishment I needed. Her thoughts were with Pa as he traveled in that cold winter. Seldom did she think of me, and then only to wish that I was not there inside her body. The coldness in her chilled me to the very soul. Body cold, soul cold. A burden to her body and a burden to the world. Why did I have to come now? I did not want to come through the veil and enter that poor impoverished home. They didn't have food for the ones they had. How could they feed another? There was no room in that small house for another child.

Many were the days when Mama would sit in front of the fireplace after the children had all gone to bed, and cry for the men who had gone. She mourned the men and then sighed for the babies who had gone on to glory. The short, cold days of winter confined Mama and the children in the cabin. The only things they went outside for were to do the chores and care for the necessities of living. The older children helped some with the chores but Mama went with them to make sure things were done properly. If she didn't watch, the boys would play and not get things done. If they forgot and left the barn door open we would lose our stock to wild animals. We needed the stock for survival, but the wild animals needed food too. Foxes came into our chicken pen and killed many of the hens that winter. Each time the chickens were raided it meant fewer eggs and the loss of meat the family needed.

War must be a terrible thing. It takes the men away and makes the women cry. Why do men go to battle? Why could they not settle differences without fighting and hurting each other? Mama fears that Pa won't come back. No one else can take his place. She needs him, not me. I can't take his place. I am only a wee, small babe. The sadness and pain were so great there in that home that my soul could not abide. The small, malnourished body could not house the soul which cried for birth. Life was not to be for the small babe.

The name on the tombstone reads:

SARAH ELIZABETH
BORN AND DIED APRIL 3,1861
SENT TO THE EARTH FOR ONE SHORT MOMENT
SPENDING ETERNITY WITH THE ANGELS

I never did see the Pa that gave me life. Only a shadow of a memory of him remains. The shadow memory of a man who conceived a child from lustful hunger but could not give her love. Life conceived in a moment of energetic outpouring of masculine seed. Conceived from need but not in love. Shall I ever find love? The loneliness and emptiness are all I feel from that short miserable existence.

33

Raise the cup of love high
to the babe conceived in lust,
formed in misery and need,
born into the coldness of a mountain cabin,
only to breathe one fleeting breath.
Never to see the light of the sun
shining full in her babies blue eyes,
never to feel a warm caress,
never to feel a kiss.

The infant who had so much to do,
so much to show the world.
The pain of that fitful, fragment of life,
holds me tight in its' mystical fist.
I want to be free of the pall that lies
over that hilltop grave,
free to leave the veil of tears
and soar to higher plains.

Away to a land where small babes find
the love and light they need.
I don't ask for riches and gold
or treasures beyond compare.
I only ask for the Master's touch
and a warm welcome home up there.

Send the love into the veil.
Break the bonds of Pain.
Free my soul to soar at last
to the Kingdom of our God.
The kingdom above
where the light never dims
and the soul of a babe finds peace.

SYBIL SPEAKS

Born to toil and hardship.
Born to care for man and the children of man.
Born to bring the Light of God to this woeful world.
Born to be a shining star on a canvas of darkness.

Women are the light of the world. The soul of woman is
sweet and kind, loving, and patient. Men's souls are brusque and
full of fire, the builders of the women's dreams.
The world needs the souls of both men and women to find
the balance ordained by God. Women dream the dreams of joy

and love, sing the lullabies, and caress the newborn babe. She teaches the children of the great God above and shows them the secrets of the earth. The Mother shows the littlest tot the king in the pansies face. The little king sitting on his throne, his crown all in place. But, look below where his feet are soaking in a tub. She picks the daisy and weaves a daisy chain to place on her princesses' heads. Her joy in the gifts of God's great earth inspire her children in the spiritual quest. Her song of praise raised heavenward at morning, noon, and night, guides the wandering soul. Her soul of purity, love, and gentle reprise, smooths the edges of lifes rigors.

I am Sybil. The Little Sisters lost much of their finer quality because they failed to look beyond the meanness of the harsh, hill country existence. The darkness and rudeness of the hewn log homes crushed upon the love of beauty. Illness, weakness and continual hardship drove the soul deep into hidden crevices. Again, I tell you that the religion of the time was not suited to the needs of women. Sermons consisted of repeated admonitions to repent from sinful ways, were male dominated and male directed. Love was not the mainstay of the religious ceremony. Conflict arose in the women because they knew, innately, the love of God, the God of New Testament understanding. Old Testament laws and beliefs were the order of the day with much accompanying misinterpretation. Many of the preachers coming into the mountains were poorly educated, rough, and cruel. Many were outcasts from society and, more than a few, fled from crimes they had committed. Preaching assured them shelter and food in exchange for a sermon. The firier and louder that sermon the better the people liked it. Fear and guilt were the maxim in those crude, unenlightened deliveries. Rare was the preacher who came driven and empowered by the Spirit of God.

My name is Sybil, too, and I, too, lived in those harsh times. Crude and rude was the life. Hardship was the rule rather than the exception. Food was scarce and of poor quality three seasons of the year. Summer brought plenty, if the rains came at the proper time and wild animals did not raid the gardens. Water was plentiful most years, but not always when we needed it. Dirt was a way of life.

It was hard not to become embittered as the drudgery and boredom ground day after day. My best defense against the deadness of soul, which occurred with so many, was to go to the woods to commune with the trees and rocks. There I would pour out my hearts desires and tell my awful secrets. The trees and rocks stood mutely by, absorbing it all, but never telling a person. When the weather was pretty I would climb a hill and look off to the mountains. The mountains gave me strength and courage. Each time I saw them they were the same, yet subtly different. Colors change from season to season, but also from day to day, and moment by moment, as light and clouds move across their wide expanse. The mountains tower there in majesty holding the secrets of time. Stern and stark against the sky, yet gentle and forgiving. Mountain country is no place for weakness, either physical or spiritual. The weak lose all to the demands of living. Steady faith and patience create the endurance necessary to live in the mountains and hills. Life is not easy. Life is not beautiful. Beauty must be found within the individual and in the world outside the four walls of the crowded cabin. Beauty lay all around for the taking. Eyes which saw beyond the mean and tawdry saw the beauty in the sky and on the ground. Ears that heard beyond the present knew the Master's voice and nature's whispered secrets. Now everyone heard the wind in the pines, but few heard the gentlest breeze lapping around the eaves.

One of the pleasures of fall was to stand on the hill behind the cabin and see the wood smoke rising from the chimney and melting into the crisp, clear fall air. If you looked you could see fairies and elves, faces, and all sorts of things in that smoke. Here for a moment and then gone, wafted away in the breeze. Strange how pleasant the smoke smelled from there and how unpleasant it smells inside the cabin in the dead of winter.

Children and adults, too, needed to get out into the fresh air, no matter how cold or wet the weather. Many brought the old country belief that night air, cold and dampness, were bad for the lungs and body in general, so they confined the children to the cabin during the winter months. Many did not have enough warm clothes to send the children outside. Poverty and ignorance of how to provide caused much of the hardship. Many ate all they could find while it was available and failed to provide for the months when none was attainable. They could not see beyond today, so did not plan.

Children were to be seen and not heard, so lost their curiosity at a young age. Many hid the desire for knowledge and understanding because of the scorn of those who did not care to learn. Too many were satisfied with the little understanding they had and were afraid to challenge what they had been told. Misinformation thus became fact, indisputable and immutable. Books were scarce and of poor quality. Many families did not even have a Bible. Peddlers coming through carried few books because few were wanted; they were costly and were too easily damaged in a pack. The added weight in a pack prohibited easy transport of books.

Everything transported into the mountains had to have purpose and function. Mountain trails, difficult to traverse at best, became impassable for many months of the year, so that, when the seasons did permit, only the necessities were brought in. There was no money to buy frivolous items. Barter and trade were the commonest mode of business transaction.

Illness presented real problems to even the hardiest mountaineers. Thrown on their own resources and knowledge passed down through the generations, they used what the earth had to offer. Indian knowledge was lost to the white settlers as they drove the Indians out of their lands. Greed and fear blocked the way to communication which would have allowed both races to live in harmony on the land. Each could have learned from the other, improving their lot and making life easier for all. Instead, men clung to the past and the ways of the Old World, in many cases, trying to make city ways work in the mountains. People who were able to adapt to the rigors and demands of the mountains survived and thrived in the hostile environment. Those who could not adapt died.

Life was harsh and hard, but the beauty of the world around compensated. Freedom was better than enslavement. The mountains answered to no man. He could find God on every side if he but looked. Families where some balance of masculine and feminine traits were found, where God was center, and where love abounded, survived and grew in the long winter months.

Beauty and love are free, not to be rationed or guarded with a miserly hand. Only those who give of these precious gifts receive in full return and grow in the wisdom of God.

NAHANA SPEAKS OF GOD

I am Nahana. I want to speak to you again. The others have given permission. It was I who was speaking for the group earlier. We were the group, the remnant who remembered the true God whose message was brought by the Fathers and Mothers. By the time I lived much of the story had been garbled and lost in misunderstanding. The original message had been preserved in the priestly line in purity. Unfortunately, the people were corrupted by the ignorance already present on earth. They chose not to follow truth so sought their own truth in things that were not of the true spirit and truth. We saw in the sun the symbolization of our great God and Creator. We did not worship the sun, but turned daily to the sun to draw its' strength into our beings. The light was similar and symbolic of the light and love of the Creator. The warmth, too, symbolized the warmth of the universal love. Without this light and warmth, death and darkness prevail. We needed the warmth and light just as you do now.

Our temples were scattered over all the earth. Ours had been a mighty world nation of peace loving peoples. Jealousy and greed had eroded the truths and separated the people into warring factions. Then as now, there were those who sought fame and fortune, to the detriment of others. Their lives became man and materially centered, rather than centering on our One

Great God. As this happened, the lives of those who followed the priestly line became endangered. People did not want to hear the truth so destroyed those who taught and lived in truth. As the destruction mounted even the edifices of the priestly line were laid waste. The corrupt did not want even the stones of the buildings to remain to manifest what had been and was now being destroyed. Buildings were desecrated, the very stones beaten into fragments and tumbled from peaks. The mysteries and secrets were buried to preserve, in some way, that which had been brought. Lives were lost. Bloodshed became a way of life.

MENANAH TAKES OVER

Yes, I lived before Nahana. She gave me permission to speak to you. I am of the ancients of whom she speaks. My name is Menanah. Yes, many of the names ended in ah. This designated the priestly line of those who came from what you call the Ice Planet. Many of the names there had the ah ending to designate home and family. We were a powerful and godly line. The name of the planet doesn't matter. The fate of the planet does matter. It matters to you now because your planet too is in danger. They did not listen to those who gave warning, the prophets. They were called prophets of doom. No one wanted to hear about doom so many did not heed. Thus the end came sooner than was anticipated and many lives were lost.

You see the remnants of the mighty temples and edifices. Continue to search the land. You won't look silly. See the truth lying all around you. Share the truth with those who can see and hear. Withhold from those who fear and do not want to hear the truth. Only a few can hear and see. Don't fear the others, and don't try to bring them with you. You cannot save all of them nor show the truth to those who do not want it. Peace to you, my love to you. You are our beloved. We raise our hands to you, you strong and courageous woman. We have sought one such as you for a long time as you count time. Your earth needs the message. We all need the message freely given for survival of all earths. Farewell, and thank you for listening. Menanah.

NAHANA TAKES OVER

Thank you for listening to Menanah. She has a good message for you and all who will listen to you. As you see, she was not and is not evil and never will be. I Nahana am not evil. I too have never been and never will be evil any more than you. We have all suffered many hurts from those who do not understand, so fear us. We protect you and others from destructive forces. We

38

want to work with you now to prevent what happened before. If we all work together in peace and love, we will be able to alter the course which the earth now follows.

Continue to use the maps and find the most powerful points. Follow the lines and draw the conclusions. We will be with you and show you what you need to know. For the sake of the future of earth don't run away. Stay with this and trust God, yourself, and us. Sybil, the legion, Nahana, all the others wish you well and want to help you. We protect you. We form a shield about you. Only mortal man can penetrate that barrier, but not for long. Continue to search. Continue to test what you are finding.

Walk uprightly and without faltering. Don't look back. Don't run back. Go forward. Seek the clues to the Riddler's Maze. You are finding more clues. You have trouble realizing the size and magnitude of the temples and edifices.

The tools used today in building are massive and cumbersome. The ancients used tools which were small and delicate but powerful. They used the energy of the earth to reconstruct the earth into forms that were pleasing to both men and the earth. As they sought the powerful points they asked permission of the earth to make changes. Thus they won the cooperation of the earth, used earth energies and built edifices which were compatible to the earth. All was in harmony. There was not discordance in the meld of earth and building. Because of this, they were able to build what now look like impossible buildings. The shapes followed earth planes, so complimented the earth and brought power from the Universe to those sites. There was an exchange at these points between earth and the Universe. Communication is powerful at these points. That is why you can hear the Little Sisters better at some points than at others.

Look at the water spots, where the water reaches the surface of the ground. Feel the energy at these spots. Rely on yourself. Seek those who know of spots that look or feel different from the surrounding terrain. You will see the pattern. You are getting closer.You are doing well. Keep on. Don't quit now. We will give you encouragement and love. Our energies are yours. We move as one in the search for the clues and answers to the Riddler's Maze.

Beloved, Shine forth in truth and life, light and love. Go in peace.

THE HEALING POOL

I have been to the spring to bathe. The waters rose from deep within the earth bringing up the power and energy of the depths. Many of us came to the spring to be healed of the diseases and problems which our race had acquired when we came to earth. The earth is not hospitable to us. We were accustomed to a rarer atmosphere and did not adapt well to the heavy atmosphere, increased pull of gravity, and the changing seasons. The memories of the Ice Planet lie heavily in our cells. The winter months create much fear and panic in the People. The ancient memories lie near the surface and are easily felt when the weather begins to cool.

During the warm months we all like to bathe in the waters of the spring to soak away the hurts and pains of the winter, both physical and mental.

So much has happened to us since that first awful time when we were forced from our homes by ice and snow. The loneliness and loss of families has created permanent scars. We shall always fear losing that which we love. The memory is so strong. All suffer the same fears because all were severed from families. Families were important at home. Many would not select one to be sent so were lost to future times. It was a hard decision that had to be made to let the young ones come. There was no choice. The young did not have a choice and the adults could not do anything to alter the necessity of sending children out to discover a new world upon which to carry on life. The civilization was too great and powerful to be lost forever. They had great knowledge in many areas. They were spiritually mature and emotionally sound. The secrets of the Universe were theirs. Since arriving on earth there has been much great hardship. Foods of the earth are inappropriate for the gentler bodies. Materials for clothing are coarse and uncomfortable in comparison to the beautiful soft materials of home. The need for heavy clothing creates a burden on the body. We have been exposed to diseases which were unknown at home and many have died because they did not have the resources necessary to fight disease. Our life span has been greatly reduced (from thousands of years). The mortality rate is high because of the gentler nature of the People. We were not prepared for such harshness of environment. Because of the rush in leaving and the necessity, or the decision, to send so many children, the messages became garbled and many lost. The adults who did come were required to care for the children more than they had been expecting so were unable to teach and compile all they needed to. As the children grew with their pieces of isolated knowledge they were unable to fit the pieces together. Thus, succeeding generations sought to use their knowledge in destructive ways. Because of fragmentation of knowledge, the true purpose was lost and adverse purposes were sought. Never was it meant for the knowledge to be used for destruction.

Ours was a peace-loving culture. We did not know the

rudiments of war or of protecting ourselves from the cruel, marauding bands of earth men. Many of the secrets were lost as the people who carried them were lost. We were forced to develop ourselves for self-protection. Thus, skills which had been used for generations of and in peace were corrupted into survival techniques and then into destructive approaches. Survival is and has been a primary concern for eons.

Since you were the first, the ancient of ancients, you understand what happened and what is happening. Never were we to know the peace of home. Never again would we have the comfort of family, with no feeling of loss. Our ties were severed so completely that many memories were shut away in only a few generations. The memories lay dormant within the genes and cells, plaguing a mighty people and bringing them down to earthly levels. The power of the earth renewed and restored a partial balance to the hurting people. Never could the comfort and balance that they had left be recaptured. The power of the earth is great in special spots where lines cross and converge. Find these lines and use them to renew and restore yourself. Strengthen them with your energy. Do an exchange with the earth. Draw from the earth but also return energy to the earth. We all groan and die with the earth. You are in a strong area. There are many converging lines and much power. You must learn how to use this power. We will direct you. Stay open. Stay attuned. Don't let the witch hunters chase you away. Use the powers which have been revealed to you. Use them for growth and strength and to help others. Lead others to find the secrets buried deep within themselves and to become attuned to the earth and to us. It is our survival.

BESS

I was one of the little ones in many ways. Born to slaves across the mountains, I was brought over the rugged trails by a family coming to homestead in the wild frontier. Harsh was my life with that family. Harsh too was their life in the cold and rugged country lying West of the great mountains. My job was to care for the children and prepare the meager food we had.

Although I worked from dawn to after dusk I still could not manage to please a harsh, cruel master. He drove his children and wife the same as he drove me and himself. His dream of riches and glory were never found as he was killed one day by a rattlesnake bite. This left Missus and me with the children. Try as we might, there was never enough food for all of us. We took turns going without so that the littlest ones could have food. Even so, the smallest two died in the first winter. The second winter took another of the younger children. We struggled

41

through the hot summers and cold winters until there was nothing left of us to struggle. Loneliness took its toll as we so seldom saw people, locked away as we were on that hilltop.

My gravestone now lies smooth to the touch but the imprint of the crudely carved letters is still there:

BESS

1684

SALLY

Hello. My name is Sarah but they called me Sally. I lived many years ago over by the mountains. Unlike many of the others, I did not find the grave a welcome relief from a miserable existence. I was loved and loved in return. I felt the love of both my parents and my family and I gave love in return. The cold winters brought a closeness to the family as we sat before the warm fire roasting chestnuts and eating apples from our own orchard. We sang the songs of our ancestors and the gospel hymns of the church. Papa had a rich, deep voice that made us all feel good. He loved to sing the songs of the Irish hills. His eyes would take on a dreamy look when he sang the songs he had learned from his old grandfather. It felt sometimes as if we could smell the heather and the gorse as he sang the old songs.

Mama would rock and dream as she listened to him. She too dreamed of the land across the sea. Unlike Papa, she remembered the land across the sea and the cold, hard trip with so many dying in the damp, dark, crowded ships. Many of her loved ones did not survive the voyage, so were buried at sea, never to see the land for which they yearned and never to realize the dream that drew them from the homeland toward an unexplored New World.

As we listened to Papa sing we could hear in his voice the warmth and love he felt for all of us and this mountain paradise we called home. He had followed the paths of the ancients and the Indians to find land on which to build a house and plant crops. He was a strong man, big and brawny. He was no stranger to work and shouldered the yoke willingly. He often said that no man deserved to eat unless he helped to grow the food. He couldn't tolerate the lazy or the whiner. Never did he send someone else to do the job that he could do himself. He was always kind and truthful, and always, always willing to answer the questions of the children. Many long winter evenings in front of the fire he told us of God and His Son Jesus. It was almost as if Papa knew them and had been there at the crucifixion, so real were his stories. He told us of the way Jesus looked, hanging there on the cross with the tears of compassion streaming down his face. Papa said that Jesus never lost His love for men even though they scorned and scoffed Him, putting Him to death on that cruel cross. Papa too would get great tears in his eyes as he told how Jesus forgave the very men who put Him to death, and how he thirsted on that dry, hot day. Papa told of how the soldiers pierced His side and freed the crimson blood, then lifted Him down and laid Him on the ground. It was almost as if Papa was one of those friends who carried the Master to the grave, cleaned the blood from His hands and side, bathed the body in sweet smelling herbs, then wrapped Him in the linen shroud. Papa told of the strain of rolling the rock across the grave opening and the grief that was felt as the men turned their backs and slowly returned to their rooms, there to mourn in awful silence. He spoke sadly and haltingly of the long, dark day in which the sealed grave held its' awful burden. And of the lost and helpless feeling the friends experienced. Lost and unsure of what to do with the message they had been given. Would they too be hanged upon a cross or banished to the wilderness because of what they knew? Fear mingled with the grief to crush them and sap away their strength. As Papa told us of that awful day, we too felt the fear and grief of those long ago followers. Would we have the strength and courage to do what those had done? I think not. I think we would have succumbed to the fear and run from our duty.

Then Papa's face would light with joy and the tears of sorrow became tears of joy as he told of the rising of our Lord. In the early hours of the day when the sun was just arising, the tomb was found empty of its' awful burden. Had the grave been robbed? What terrible thing had befallen our Master? Then the truth broke forth in clarity. The tomb had not been strong enough to hold that wonderful man. He had broken free of the shackles of the shroud of death and walked victorious on the land. He had conquered the grave and all mankind. He had foiled the executioners plan. Never again would the grave hold that man!

Then Papa would lean back, close his eyes and in solemn wonder state, "The greatest man that ever lived walked the soil, breathed the air, felt the rain, and felt the pain, just the same as you and I. He knew a woman's warm caress. He heard the baby's cry. He felt the fear of cowardly men and the pain of an awful death. But He never once turned His back on men. He loved us then and He loves us now. The least we can do is to love Him, the Father and all His creation. Jesus didn't complain when he had a task to do and neither shall we."

Mama, sitting with eyes closed, would nod in agreement,

"Yes Rob," she would say, "you are so right. The Master asks us all to do His will and live each day for him. Our home here in the hills is His. To Him be the glory and the honor."

As the dying embers cast shadows into the darkened corners of the cabin, we would all bow our heads together, join hands and pray, "Our Father which art in heaven." Even the little ones learned this prayer before all others. Small voices lisped, "Hallowed by thy name. Thy kingdom come. Thy will be done on earth as it is in heaven." Thy will be done, how simple that sounds. On earth as it is in heaven. How do I know how it is in heaven? Then Papa would hear my voice lagging behind the others and give me a soft nudge.

"Give us this day our daily bread." Today He was good to us. He gave us meat and potatoes, apples and chestnuts to eat with our bread. He gave us fresh cold water from the spring and warm milk from the cow . . . Papa's nudge again.

"And forgive us our trespasses as we forgive those who trespass against us." How can we trespass when there aren't any neighbors for miles and miles?

"Lead us not into temptation." Papa always gives an extra hug on this one because he knows I have trouble keeping my mind on what the others are saying.

"But deliver us from evil." How could evil come to our hill paradise? What does evil look like? Does it have hair all over like the bears or does it crawl on the ground like the snakes? I hope I never see evil.

"For thine is the kingdom, and the power and the glory forever. Amen."

Then it is kisses and hugs all around and all the children climb the ladder to the loft to sleep. The bed is cold in the winter and hot in the summer. In the winter I like to sleep in the middle between Eleanor and Mary so they can keep me warm. But in the summer I like to sleep on the outside where it is cooler. The boys sleep on the other side of the opening where it is colder. We girls are lucky because our bed is beside the chimney. This keeps us warm most of the night. The loft is nice with Mama's herbs hanging from the ceiling and smelling so good. It is especially cozy when the rain falls on the roof and we can hear the wind blowing in the pines. We are so fortunate to have this beautiful home among the hills.

Mama says that where she came from it is dirty and crowded with many people living in one house. I wouldn't like that. She says the children can't go out to play because the streets are dangerous and dirty. Men riding by on horses don't watch for little children so let their horses hurt them. Water and dirt in the streets make a terrible smell and the noise is unpleasant. She says she was always hungry because there wasn't enough food for all the people and there was no place to grow it in the city. The food they did have was not good, often being rotten or vermin infested. She tells us to thank God daily for our warm cabin and the space to help ourselves. We are never to complain about the cold or about not having what we want to eat. She says to be thankful for what we have and not to go wanting something different.

Death came suddenly, silently, and inexorably to all of us one cold, snowy, windy winter night. The weather had been cold through December and January so we had to keep the fires going hard all winter. On a night in February when the trees creaked and groaned with the cold, a stray spark of fire found a dry timber on the floor. Slowly and stealthily the cabin filled with smoke. Sleeping eyes remained closed never again to open. Quiet lips kept their secrets. Smoke filled lungs stopped their labors and pounding hearts were stilled. Death lay solemnly and serenely on the cabin before the flames reached their zenith. Painless death, the sleep that never wakens, the joys of life sealed in eternity.

By morning all that remained of our hill cabin was the chimney standing starkly against the sky, the doorstep and the smoldering remains of a joyous and loving family.

Mourn not those who have gone before.
Cry not the tears of grief.
We fled the mortal life on earth
For a spirit world of bliss.

Never ask the repeated why.
Just know that all must die.
Life goes on in the physical realm
Without those who have gone before.
But, the spirit world lies just beside
With the joys and pleasures multiplied.

Sing your songs of gladness
Sing your songs of bliss
Raise the cup of gladness
Send a tender kiss.
Fear not the grim reaper's blade,
Fear not when life is o'er.

Your life of eternal joy
Awaits those whose life is made.
Rest on the great, grand promise
Of the Master's great command.
Love and give life meaning
As you approach the golden strand.

Weep not for the little children.
Weep not for the old and grey,
For theirs' is the grand tomorrow
Which comes with the brand new day.

Death holds no sting.
Death holds no misery.
Death is a bright new passage
Into a land of mystery.

Our Master holds the secret
Of our eternal bliss.
Our Master made the promise
And sealed it with a kiss.

Look upward and move onward.
Doubt not your role in time.
Earth binds the spirits closely,
But gives us life sublime.

Know the peace of wisdom
Seek for life's deep secrets.
The Universe unfolds to those
Who search and seek her secrets.

Look to God for comfort.
Look to God for balm.
Life's struggles overcome
God leads us to the calm.

Seek in higher places
The secrets of the ages.
Fear not the scorn of mankind.
But seek through myriad stages.

Life, the eternal question,
Life, the Riddler's Maze.
Life the greatest gift of all
To hold within our gaze.

Life, a step in eternity
Use it, seek it, cherish it.
Never run away in fear and doubt.
Stay, until the quest is won.

BETSY

Betsy is my name. Betsy Nora Lee. My home is in the valley where the tall pines grow. The river waters our land with ever flowing waters. Never do we want for water on our valley farm. Everywhere, the daisies, cornflowers, and sunflowers grow. Papa runs a sawmill to cut the great trees into boards to build a town. Many people are moving over the mountains to settle by the river. I don't like for the people to come and settle by the river. It crowds our little farm and steals our quiet and solitude. Each morning we hear the rasp of saws and pounding of nails as people prepare for the winter months. Papa likes for the people to come because it keeps him busy and helps him make money. Much of his work is done for barter, but Papa prefers money. That he can hide away and "save for a rainy day." I don't know what he means by that because we have lots of rainy days and we don't use the money on either rainy or sunny days.

Papa says the love of money is the root of all evil, but that doesn't seem to bother him. I guess his love is alright and not evil.

One day when Mama went to the river to wash clothes, a group of Indians came by and asked for food. Said they were on their way to a happier place where the white man didn't crowd in. They knew which trails to follow and where they were headed. Mama told them we didn't have food for pagan savages so to get on their way. Seemed strange to me that she wouldn't share with these hungry people. They didn't look either pagan or savage to me. They looked sad and hungry to me. The little children looked with great, sad, brown eyes at the houses being built where the great trees had been cut away. As they passed along, the misery was there to see. Were these the proud, cruel people that the old men had warned us about? How could these beaten and starving people ravage a white man's settlement? They looked as if they had traveled far and felt the weariness and hunger of a lost and lonely people. Where were the war paint and the throbbing drums that signaled war? Had the guns of war silenced a mighty song? Could we not have lived in harmony with these seeking, lonely people? Why did they have to pass on to find a resting place? Could they not have built a home along our river bank? Why must they travel into lands beyond the hills? As they passed away from view, I waved a sad farewell for the weary, defeated remnant of a once proud and mighty tribe. How unjust our ways. How cruel the powers of greed.

I am having difficulty with the telling of my life story. So much was happening in that growing settlement beside the river. I want to tell it all but know that it can't all be told. Life changed quickly as travelers came and went, many staying in our mountain valley town. In the spring, when the rains came, mud covered the land, making work hard. Many people came through the mud and rain to start building early so that they would have a warm home for winter. People coming from the cities didn't know how to select their land, plant their crops, or build a house. Many died before they could make the proper preparations to live. Children died of disease and exposure, improper food and from the dirt that was everywhere.

Summer was a time of frantic activity as so much had to be done before the cold winter months began. I like summer except for the flies and bugs. It feels good to run barefoot through the grass and wade in the shallows of the river. I like to sit by the river and watch the drovers fording the river with their herds of cattle. Wagons carrying goods cross the river in the town as they pass through heading west. Families, too, pass through in the search for land and homes. Women and children trudge wearily along beside the wagons to lighten the load. I see many sad-eyed women walking with weary, stooped shoulders, mourning the homes and families they have left behind as they follow the men into the mountains. Blank faces, too, poorly mask the sadness of the women. Children with dust-streaked faces show the strain and toil of the long journey. Many would like to stop and stay but are pushed relentlessly onward by the dreams of the fathers who seek and yearn for land of their own. There they plan to build a home and life for their impoverished families who have fled the hardships of a crowded existence.

Peddlers come to town selling their wares. Such beautiful things they bring! Needles, and thimbles, thread and cloth for beautiful dresses, knives and scissors, pots and pans. I like to see the treasures of the peddler as he lays out his stores of pepper, salt, cinnamon and other spices from around the world. Sometimes he carries a strip of lace or ribbon for some lucky lady's dress. I never had lace or ribbons on my dresses, but I do think it would be so pretty! Papa says we don't need these frivolous things, that they don't keep us warm or dry. Just the same, I think it would be nice to have something pretty on my dress. One day a peddler had the most beautiful picture of a man holding a sheep. It said, "The Good Shepherd." I wanted that picture to take home with me to look at when I went to bed and when I got up in the morning. It was just a little picture and only cost a penny, but, Papa said, "No, we don't need that kind of nonsense around our house." Plead as I might, he wouldn't change his mind. I did so want that little picture of the kind-faced man. Not many men I see have a kind face like that. I don't really think Papa is a mean, cruel man, but he sure doesn't cotton to fancy things or pretty things, either. He says that is a waste of hard-earned money and we don't need that kind of frivolity. It sure isn't good to eat or drink, won't keep us warm, so isn't worth anything. He tells us to forget that kind of trappin's and think of practical things. It would be nice to have something pretty though.

Papa didn't hold much with church goin' either. Says that people that go to church are wastin' good time they could be spendin' workin'. He works everyday of the week and makes us work too. Says that only lazy, good for nothin's need a day of rest. He says God ain't nothin' anyhow. That all that's a waste of time that can be spent for better purpose. Some Sundays, when I'm out workin' in the garden and the windows of the church house are open, I can hear the singin' spreading out all over the valley. It mingles with the sound of the river and echoes back from the hills. I like to hear the singin'. It sounds so happy. If Papa catches us listenin' he gives us a tongue lashin' and tells us to get back to work, that the weeds are growin' faster than we can pull them out. Someday I would like to have a pretty dress, nice new shoes, a ribbon for my old dusty looking bonnet, and go up to the church house with the other people, to sit in the pews and sing. I don't know what else goes on in that church house, but the singin' would be such fun that it wouldn't matter what else was done. Mama says there's preachin' that goes on, but I don't understand what that would be. When I ask her she says, "Hush up! Don't ask all those infernal questions. Can't you see I'm busy? Get your work done." It doesn't do much good to ask Mama questions. She doesn't have time to answer. Papa acts like he doesn't even hear, so I don't ask him. He can't see any reason to learn more than we need to for gettin' the work done.

The summer I died was hot and dry. The river ran low and dirty. Along the banks the green slime grew. Each new day the sun rose hot and scorched the land. The grass turned brown before its time and the gardens shriveled before they produced. As the heat of the sun reached into my dark, shuttered room, it burned into my fevered body, battling to see which was hotter. As the summer complaint grew worse, I could feel my body parching with dryness. Vital and life sustaining fluids poured from my body in the sweaty heat. Death came as a welcome relief from the heat and filth.

As I lay alone in the dark and lonely room, I thought back to that little picture card of the peddler's so long before and wondered if I would ever see a face so kind and pure. I wondered if I would ever sing or have a pretty ribbon. Does life have to be so practical? Is every task a chore? Can there be no beauty for Betsy Nora Lee? Why must I do without knowing that good shepherd? But, then, perhaps I will meet that good shepherd who cares about his sheep. Perhaps I'll find a ribbon and pretty frivolous things. Beauty lay all about all the years of my miserly life, but none was invited in. Today, I invite it in. Papa can't touch the beauty that lies within as I leave this fevered, feverish existence. So sad it is that he can't see the beauty and seek the joy in those songs from the church house.

Good-bye, Papa. I go to a beautiful place where all is peace and rest and the Good Shepherd smiles His loving smile. I will not miss the toil and labor, nor your pinched and impoverished ways. My soul breaks free of the earthbound mass and soars to a brand new home. Farewell to toil, farewell to confusion and pain. I go to a higher plane.

MAGGIE

My name is Margaret but they called me Maggie. My life here in the mountains was hard, but pleasant. We were tillers of the soil in the deep valley between the hills. Our valley was broad and fertile. The fields were level and almost barren of rock.

When I was young Pa would lift me on the back of our old horse Sam, hitch the plow behind and I would ride back and forth plowing the field. Then he would change the plow for the harrow and back we would go to break up the clods. Now and then Pa called, "Whoa" and we stopped so that Pa could gather the rocks and put them on the harrow. It seemed that every spring a few rocks had worked up out of that soil. We added them to the pile around the spring. Following the harrowing he put the drag on behind the horse and we went back and forth again, smoothing the soil until it was fine and even. Then Pa would take the old corn planter that his Grandpa had made, strap it to his leg, and go walking out across the field. The corn planter was a piece of metal rolled into a cone shape and then strapped to his leg. He would walk along, push the end of that cone into the ground, then place three or four kernels of corn into the hole, raise his foot which lifted the cone and go on to plant the next hill. Pa did this real well. His Grandpa had taught him how to make the rows even in all directions. Grandpa had taught him how to step just right so that the whole field looked like a giant checkerboard. When the corn was tall you could walk those rows from any direction, up, down, back, forth, and even catty-cornered. He sure knew how to make that field look pretty.

I liked riding old Sam back and forth through the field. His back was big and broad and he never tripped or missed a step. Sometimes on hot days the harness and Sam's sweat rubbed my legs, but on those days Pa would say that Sam needed rest. We would stop under the shade tree at the end of the field, Pa would lift me down so I could stretch my legs and we would have a cool drink of water from the crock that Ma brought to us. Sam would stand there in the shade with his great, gentle eyes almost closed, switching flies with his tail. I loved to watch him twitch his muscles to shoo the flies on his withers and back. I always wondered how he could stand so still and twitch just one little spot. The flies would buzz up, but not for long, then settle down to rest and walk on his shiney, sweaty coat. Old Sam was a gentle, agreeable horse. He always did what we asked of him and never made complaint. Course, we never asked him to do more than he was able to and we gave him plenty of time to rest. Pa always said that the best way to get a horse, or a man, to do a job well was to know what he could do, ask him to do what he could do well, don't push for more than he is able to do, praise him often, and give him what he needs to eat. It worked for Old Sam and anyone else who came to help Pa.

I loved to ride that old horse there in the field with Pa, I liked to feel the sun on my back, then on my face, to smell the fresh dirt and the sweat on Sam. When I went home in the evening and went in the house Ma always said, "Whew, Maggie my love, you smell like a horse." She never did understand that that is my very favorite smell. The smell of horse sweat mingled with sunshine and fresh dirt is the best perfume in the world. I heard in town one time that in Paris, France, they make perfume that smells like flowers, and all the great ladies wear it. I don't know why they would want to wear something like that when they could smell like Sam, fresh dirt, and sunshine. Do you? I never could understand the ways of the fine ladies.

Sometimes Ma would get a Godey's Ladies Book and we would look at the pictures of the fine ladies in their fancy laces and feathered hats. You know they didn't look one bit comfortable. It would seem to me that they would be happier and more comfortable if they would take off all that fancy stuff that looked too stiff to sit down in and just ride a good old horse like Sam.

When I got tired from the riding and the sunshine, I could slide my legs 'long Sam's broad back, hook my arms around his collar and just go to sleep. That was like sleeping in a great big cradle as he walked swaying along.

In the summer Pa hooked Sam to a mower and I would ride along as he cut the hay. Some days were so hot that during the hottest part of the day I would lie under the trees by the spring and not ride old Sam. He sweated too much in the heat and made my legs sore, so I would go to the cool spring and watch the clouds go by. Did you ever watch clouds go by on a day when the sky is very blue? I think this is the pleasantest thing to do. You see ships, and fleecy sheep, dragons and dream castles. Sometimes the clouds look like grouchy old men with great pointy noses and sometimese like babies in their mother's arms.

When I got tired of looking at clouds and seeing all the shapes, I turned over and watched the living things on the ground in front of my eyes. There were ants scurrying about looking for food, and all sorts of interesting things that we don't see as we walk along. Did you ever wonder how an ant can pick up something bigger than he is and carry it in his little hands? Or why they carry it over their heads? Aren't they funny the way they struggle and struggle to carry something much bigger than they are and how they run around so fast? They run hither and yon, never seeming to know where they are going and how long they will stay. Or they line up and march like soldiers. They never really seem to know where they are going, though.

Another thing I liked to do was hunt for crawdads. The best way to do that is to pull up your skirt, high enough that it won't get wet, and wade slowly and carefully into the creek . Then you creep very quietly and gently up to a big flat rock, reach down very slowly, get a hold of that rock and ease it up. Sometimes you will find a great big crawdad lying there in the cool water waiting for his lunch to come floating by. Sometimes if you sit on the bank and watch, the crawdads will come out to see what you are doing. They are timid, but curious, little creatures. They can move so fast that they are there in plain sight and then gone, hidden from sight, at the least movement.

Sometimes when I go to the creek to look for crawdads I see snakes. If I go quietly and carefully I see them lying on the rocks sunning themselves. They never stay around to pass the time of day, but slither right off into the water, to lie there and look at me with their little round eyes. It is almost as if they dare you to come into their water as they stare right back.

One day I caught one of those snakes and took it to the house to show Ma. Now I thought she would like that snake the way I did, but was I wrong! When she saw that snake she started to yell and scream to get it out of her sight. I didn't see why it was so terrible and had to be out of her sight. But when Ma yells and screams like that I do what she says and don't stop to ask why. Anyway, when she got calmed down she told me I wasn't ever to bring a snake in the house again, nor toads, frogs, bugs, moths, crawdads, buttereflies, or wounded birds. Nothing that was fun and nice to have around. I don't know why I am supposed to be a lady. That doesn't look like fun at all. She wants me to be polite and mannerly and, sit prim and proper, the way it shows in Godey's Ladies Book. I can't imagine why she wants that. It just doesen't seem right to me to kill your spirit by dressing up in stiff, ugly clothes that you can't run in or lie on your belly on the ground, or wade a creek, or ride old Sam. Does it to you? It just doesn't seem right to take a free and happy spirit and push it into a stern and rigid way of acting. I don't ever want to be locked up like that!

As the years passed and life took on new responsibility my spirit never was confined. Ma tried to tame the restless soul, but to no avail. She wanted a little lady in lace and frills, but try as I might, I couldn't keep those fancy dresses clean. I would fall in a creek and get all wet or step in mud and splash it on my skirt, or just walk along and the dirt would just jump right up and get on me.

Ma finally gave up the struggle to make me a lady, but never did give up the hope. She had a hard time in our hill-farm way of living, never satisfied with what we had. She yearned for the "finer things," she called them, that she saw in Godey's Ladies Book. She never did get far from home and never did get to see all the splendors that drew mind and spirit away from the mountains. We didn't have the money nor the means to go to see the things she wanted to see. In the later years of her life she sat on the porch, just rocking back and forth, with a far-away look in her eyes. The weakness, it was called. When Pa and I were alone, out of her hearing, he would say, "Maggie, my love, never yearn for something you can't have. Be content with what you have. Love the earth and the life on it so that the weakness doesn't overcome you." It was sad to see this once proud woman caught up in the dreams of what could never be.

The weakness didn't catch up with me or none of my children. They, too, loved the smell of the earth and the feel of rain. We spent many lazy summer afternoons lying on our backs in the sun watching the sky or hunting for crawdads in the creek. We dreamed of castles and princesses and knights on white chargers, but, when the sun turned crimson in the west, we laid the dreams aside for the blessing of our happy hills. How could one hope for a more wonderful place than our farm among the hills? Here we had the freedom to breathe God's good air, to look at God's great sky, to look into the tiniest world of the ants in their frenzy, to pick a flower, to watch the lightning flash and hear the thunder roll. Why would anyone want to trade all that for a city across the sea where perfumed men and women stand gracelessly and awkwardly in their laced and pompadoured stance? Not for me the cardboard smile and miles and miles of lace. I would rather have the smell of earth, the sound of rainfall, the feel of a small furry kitten than all the glories of Paris.

In my later years, I, too, sat on the porch and rocked. But not for me the far-away look, the glazed and glassy eyes. No, never, there was too much to see in our mountain paradise. I filled my eyes with the mountains in all their moods, watched the birds flying by, the deer, the grouse, the chickadee, the wrens in their nests and the butterfly. I looked into the sky and saw the infinite blue that reaches clear to heaven. My heart sought to encompass all I saw, to carry it indelibly into eternity.

Upon the day of final rest I looked into the Master's face and heard him say, "Well done, thou good and faithful servant. In you am I well pleased," then I slipped away in peace. I do not regret my life on earth but remember it with pleasure and pride that I knew the love of God and man and, through my children, gave the earth new life.

Now I guard the seeker on his path and point the way to God. I share with God the love of earth so am allowed to guide earth's men. My earthly joy is my eternal joy, at peace in the great I Am.

DOROTHY

I am Dorothy, Dottie, Dot. Who knows which I am? The one who wants to be friendly calls me Dot. The one who wants to be intimate calls me Dottie, those who prefer formality call me Dorothy. Dorothy Imogene to be exact. I don't care which they call me because inside, where my real self lives, I call myself Myanah. Only the world knows me by Dorothy. In the Universe I am Myanah.

I was with you when we made the voyage from the Ice Planet. I was one of the children who suffered the pain of leaving home and family, only to find more pain in the alien, hostile environment of earth. The savages who made life so unbearable for us ruined the Great Plan. I was there with you on the ship and was in your care after we landed. You have seen me in this life from the life in the earliest time. I was one of the little ones who played on the beach while you watched. I loved the beach and the warmth of the sun after the cold of the Ice Planet and the cold of the ship. When the savages attacked us, we did not know what to do so ran into the forest. There the savages found us and took us to their homes where we were forced to live with their children. Little did they realize how large we would become and how slowly we matured. As we outgrew their children in size they were angry that we needed more food, so drove us out of their camps. Alhough the camps were crude and filthy, life in the jungle was harder. Wild animals preyed on us injuring and killing many. We were so helpless before them! We did not know how to defend ourselves either against the savage men or against the wild beasts. Our idyllic life on the Ice Planet, our young age, and our debilitated condition made us easy prey for the hungry beasts. Death in the cruel jungle was welcome, a relief from the hunger and fear.

Later I returned as Dorothy. Again my life was short and unfulfilled. My mission then was the same as earlier, I was to be the bearer of sons. Neither time was I to fulfill this mission. I did not live long enough to enjoy the pleasures of adulthood and motherhood. Too soon the call of the grim reaper came to free me from the strife of life.

As Dorothy I came to the hill country from which the high mountains could be seen clearly. My home was crude and barren of all pleasantries. Food was scarce and never adequate. I will probably spend my entire eternity feeling the hunger of my aborted existences on earth.

During the travail of birth my mother suffered grievous problems and I was born without the ability to communicate. I was labeled dumb or ignorant and cast aside as unsuitable to live. It was expected that I would die immediately after birth. Not so! I was not ready to fight my way back through the pall of tears hanging over that hill house. Night after night I struggled to breathe in the closeness of that crowded cabin. Each morning when day came and I was still there my parents cursed the day that I was born. Just another mouth to feed with no hope that I would ever be able to work and earn my keep.

Inside my frail body a tortured mind struggled for expression. No one, no one would listen or help me use the little skill left in my damaged brain. When neighbors came to visit, I was hustled away to the loft so that I could not be seen. When the family went to meeting or to town, I was locked in the cabin with only a crust of bread to eat. They didn't want to waste food on such as I. While they were gone, I would push a chair to the window, climb up and watch the world within my view. Seldom was I allowed the privilege of going into that sunlit world.

As I grew my body matured into that of a woman. Pa liked that. He would come to me at night and use my body for practices meant only for the wife. He would hold his hand over my mouth so that I could not cry out and lunge himself onto and into my body. Over and over his body would rock over mine as I lay there helpless under his cruel weight. His animal lust sated, he would go back to his own bed and sleep the sleep of the satisfied animal that he was. Never was I asked if I wanted his lustful attention. Never was I given choice. Only his desire was satisfied while I lay dying beneath his clutch.

Seldom did I hear my name in that cold, indifferent world. Once the preacher came, and I was called Dorothy to him. They told him I was Dorothy but didn't have a dot of brain. Everyone laughed at that. It really wasn't funny, you know. Why did they act as if I didn't know anything? Little did they know!

Pa thought it funny when the neighbor boys came by and saw me with my woman's body. "For two bits you can bed Dottie," he would say. Those dirty, stinking boys would give the two bits and use my body the way Pa did. How I hated the pain and humiliation of that terrible act. Panting and sweating they attacked me over and over while Pa stood by and laughed, never noticing my tear filled eyes. One after another they came until all were satisfied, then they would leave me with that terrible man, his animal instincts at a feverish pitch. When finally he would quit my body, there was no strength left in me to even cry. The pain of my body was as nothing beside the pain in my soul.

One day I felt new life within my own and knew that another girl baby was to be born. Never would I, never could I permit another young girl's soul to live the life that I had. Easy it was to end the lives of my daughter and myself. The river ran close to the house. While no one looked, I slipped away and ran to the cool, clean river. I walked into that cool, clean water until it rose around my knees. On I walked until it rose around my hips and washed away the sin-stained men's excretion. Up to the breasts the water came and cleansed the hurts of where men's hands had mangled. Up to the neck, cool and sweet, the cleansing water rose. When finally I stepped in over my head, the cool water cleansed the suffocating filth of the cabin's dirt from deep within my lungs.

The small life within my own struggled for only a trice, then flew away to a better place, where God cares for the smallest one. My own death was sweet as I felt the cleansing wash. Death, sweet death of the body so sorely used. My soul set free, the bondage broken, my home on earth no more. Away I soared with the unborn soul to find a place of eternal rest.

"Poor fool," they said. "Why did she go and do that terrible thing.?"

"Poor man," they said of my cruel Pa. "He loved his daughter SO."

The boys in the neighborhood stood round and laughed at the fun they'd had. Not one of them knew that a small new soul lay deep in my woman's body. Free at last from man's cruel lusts, free to think and speak to the great I Am. Free to soar from this pain-wracked earth and sit at the Master's feet. I'll never walk this way again. I'll never seek to return. Earth, so cruel, so very cruel, I flee your clutching, panting, throbbing body of men to live in eternal bliss. Earth, home of man, I bid you farewell, I and my little one.

MARGIE

My name is Margie, and I lived over by the high mountain beside a cool stream. Always in the summer I liked to watch the birds fly and hear the bees singing as they went about their work. Pa was a miller so we had lots of people near our door. Farmers with great heavy bags of corn and wheat, came daily to our mill to have the grain ground into fine, pure flour. Sometimes they brought their wives and children with them, and I had someone to play with. It was fun to watch their gentle horses lazing in the sun, switching flies with their long, stringy tails.

Our house adjoined the mill so we were always there and

always had plenty of flour, since part of the pay was in grain. We fed our chickens and horse with the grain the farmers left in payment.

Life could have been pleasant there in the mill by the creek, but there was a sadness and a loneliness that permeated everything in that valley. Often, when I went to bed at night, I would hear the crying of an Indian maiden mourning her long lost brave. At other times I could hear the wail of an ancient mother mourning her sick and dying child. Why are women born to sorrow? Why are women born to pain? Have you considered all this? Why do women feel the pain of childbirth and the sorrow of laying babies in the grave? Why is life so unjust? Will we never feel the bliss of joy, pure, free, untarnished by grief and sorrow? Are we forever destined to see joy only as a fleeting shadow, here, borne on a breeze, and then gone in a twinkling?

God, in His mercy, surely did not wish this upon His little daughters. Why do we hold to this bed of pain? Are we destined to never leave the pain wracked world, but to walk forever on the cruel, cold stones of hatred and greed? War, the mockery that man perpetrates, leaves the women kneeling at the graves of the thwarted lives of the sons torn loose from her aching arms. Why can not peace the pattern be? Men fight the wars and glory in battle while women carry the scars of the losses.

Never, in all my short life, could I find the answers to the questions which perplexed my days. "Margie," they'd say, "what does it matter? Where did you get these strange ideas? Run and play." How can you play when the soul sheds its tears and languishes in the breast? Why don't the others ask these questions? Do they not feel the pain? Do they not hear the voices of the mourning, sobbing sisters? Why do they scoff and turn their backs when I ask the simplest question? Why do they scorn and call me names when I stop to listen to the whispers in the breeze? Is something wrong with me? Or is it wrong with them? Why can't they hear the mournings and the loud and soulful wails? Are they deaf to all God's children or only to those beyond the veil? Can they not see the strong, clasped hands that hold the child's in death? Do they not see the Indian maid with the flowers in her hair? The maid who mourns her long lost brave.

Ma calls me strange and tells me not to ask, Pa looks away and murmurs, "How foolish." Liz and Eleanor run out to play and tell me to go to the woods by myself. They have no time for such as I. They can't see the wild goose fly. How could they see the Indian Maid? They never stop to hear the song of the bee or to watch a robin brush its wings. When they go to the woods they whoop and scream and scare the animals away. They never see the deer drinking by the stream nor the raccoons and rabbits play. Once I tried to show them a sprite in the tree beside the head," the old men say, as I listen to the sounds of another world. But, I have to ask for the millionth time, who is tetched in the head, them or I? Why can't they see and here what I see and hear? It's there plain as day. Why don't they look? I've seen angels and cathedrals come from the sky. I've seen God and His Son Jesus smile at me. The preacher says this cannot be. Why can't he see? Doesn't he look? Is he afraid of what he might see and hear? He sings of the great Hallelujah Day when he will meet Jesus face to face, but closes his eyes to the truth beside him. How often I've seen him smile and say, "We'll all get to heaven some day." How can he get to heaven when he can't see it lying all around him? Where does he think he will go? Is it some far off space out of the reach of man? Is that what he seeks? Why can't he see that heaven lies all around?

Life became to cruel as the word spread about the crazy girl, the miller's daughter. Pas' fear and Mas' scorn became more than I could bear. One summer day I went to the mountain and looked into the sky. The gates of heaven opened wide and the great God said, "Come unto me. I will give you rest." My soul slipped free of its earthly shackles and fled to the Master's arms. He gathered my tortured, battered soul into His warm embrace. He covered my shame with His loving grace and gave me the great Amen. "Well done, my little one," He said, "You lived your life of woe. You brought the truth to a blinded world. They could not see. Stay now with me." My body looked so small and frail, so hollow and forlorn, as it lay upon the rocky ground. I bid my earthly home farewell, I gave my body to the earth, My soul set free, the shackles gone, I live in the spirit world. Life on earth was death for me. Here in the world of soul set free I live, I live through eternity.

Margie

RACHAEL

Rachael wants to speak to you. My name is Rachael. I know how you feel. I, too, had a hard task to do in a time before you. I, too, met opposition and repression. I, too, knew of the mysteries, but was not allowed to speak. I was one of those who was burned at the stake. Fools! Fools! Little did they know that I told them of the true God who gives all the gifts. They saw me as a witch and possessor of demonic powers because I could call down the healing power. I knew what you know, that only God can heal. The healing that comes through Satan is short-lived and temporary. The only meaning in it is to draw people away from God. The healing does not last and the illness comes back tenfold when the fool's head has been turned. Only God gives the permanent healing.

Many of those who have sought and now seek elsewhere cannot recognize the difference between God and Satan. They have given to much power to Satan. He cannot operate without power that foolish men give him. Without foolish men he is nothing. Evil cannot hold on where good is complete.

The pain at the stake is fleeting and temporary. It freed me from physical bonds and allowed me to go to the Father. For this I am eternally grateful. This is sort of an inside joke; eternally grateful. We can only be eternally grateful when we experience eternity. Those who do not experience eternity cannot understand and appreciate eternal gratitude. They would see the death at the stake as just that, death. Instead, it was a release from the physical bonds that held me to earth and in the grounded dimension. Heaven lies at your fingertips for those who can see. Those who are able to free the soul on the temporal plane look into eternity, see infinity. As long as physical life exists, the soul is drawn back as by a magnet and cannot be freed to move into the farthest reaches. Death breaks the bonds that hold the soul as prisoner, breaks the bonds and allows total freeing, thus total freedom to search. I love this freedom. Never again do I want to be placed back into the physical bonds. You, too, will love the freedom and the vastness of that which is available to the freed soul. Waste not your earthly time on that and those which block and hold your mind in bondage. Flee those who drain you of life; who need your life blood. Seek beyond the enslaved-enslaving, entrapped-entrapping, bound-binding. Move to the higher plane. Free yourself to soar with the eagles. Lift yourself beyond the critics and jailers. Life is so short, so temporal, only a hiatus in the eternal scheme of things. Why do you worry about the physical things? What does it matter what you eat or wear? What does it matter how much money your business makes or how many people you meet and convert? You are responsible for your own destiny. Don't give up your own destiny because of the pressures of an earthly existence. How narrow and mundane, how crimped and cramped men's lives are. You there in the mountains find it hard to see beyond your noses. What you can not feel and see, you think does not exist. You are wrong. There is so much to see, so much that you are not aware of. Why do you look as if through a hunting scope? What a narrow view this gives! Broaden your vision. Look beyond the mundane. Come out of the tunnel of your own ignorance and misunderstanding. Move to new realms.

MYNON

A Vision Described

Mynon is coming from a doorway in the side of a temple that stands high on a hill. This temple is beautifully majestic in the moonlight. In his arms he is carrying a box that appears to be fairly heavy. He walks down a stairway to the left of the building to a pier where a boat is docked. He puts the box into the boat, gets in himself in the darkness, and rows away over the water. A slight silver glint sparkles on the water from a waning moon. He rows to a hill to the east where he lands and carries the box up along a roadway around the side of the hill. He approaches a large building made of stone. He approaches from the rear, stealthily. The building looks like a large stone fortress of some sort.

A door in the rear opens to Mynon. There is light in the room which he enters, still carrying the box. He seems to be in the kitchen of the large building. There is a large fireplace and a large wooden table. The room is dark around the light, seems well appointed and capable of serving the function for which it was prepared. Mynon sets the box on the table. Others gather around to look at the box. It seems that he has brought it from the temple to put it in a safe place. The others are sympathizers and helpers. They stand looking at the box and discussing its contents or purpose until a door in the left back wall of the room opens and a hooded figure enters. He looks like a monk or priest in a deep red cowl. He enters with his hands folded and head bowed in a reverent position. As he approaches the head of the table, he pushes back the hood of his cowl to reveal a young man with lightly tanned skin, blue eyes, and very light, golden brown hair, almost blond. He is quite pleasant and intelligent looking. He approaches the table and looks at the box then leans his hands on the table to look more closely at the box. There is a feeling of awe in the room, as if they are all in the presence of something holy.

The young man, Likhana, leans forward and removes something from the box. It is a large crystal ball of purest clarity. It glows in the light of the room with a pure white glow. As Likhana lifts the ball high overhead, the glow broadens and gleams. As the light brightens, the globe rises into the air and floats over the center of the table. All the men watch it raptly, gazing upward as if awestruck and caught in its spell. The ball quivers and pulsates, then sends rays of blue light out to all the men, then seems to concentrate a golden orange light on the table.

One by one the men lie down on the table and the globe moves over them shedding the golden light. As the light passes over the man on the table he is absorbed into the globe. Likhana remains at the head of the table with his hands raised throughout. He seems to be controlling the globe.

As the men enter, the globe becomes cloudy for a short time, as if filled with a mist, and then clears. The next man lies down on the table and is drawn up. There is no struggle. All are doing this of their own accord, willingly and reverently. It seems to be a permanent thing. As if they are returning home. The last man, has been elevated and the ball dims. Likhana alone remains with eyes transfixed and his arms raised. The globe darkens and floats back into the box. Likhana closes the lid and picks up the box which he carries to a raised stone on the floor of the same room. He descends a stone stairway into a dimly lighted tunnel.

The lights along the wall shine with a greenish glow and cast no shadow. The light is soothing and gentle, not harsh. Likhana moves effortlessly, but quickly down along the descending tunnel. Finally, he comes to a door at the end of the tunnel. It looks like a large wooden door with panels. It is a heavy door of a dark wood.

Likhana opens the door and steps into a room with rows of boxes, similar to the one he is carrying, on shelves around the room. He places the box he carries into a niche in the rear wall, turns and leaves the room. He takes a key from his robe and locks the door behind him. He then walks back up the tunnel, up the stairs, lowers a handle on the wall and a stone slides across the opening. When it is in place it is indistinguishable from the rest of the floor. The handle returns to the wall and blends with the wall. It, too, is indistinguishable from the rest of the wall. Likhana returns to the table, checks to make sure there are no signs of the men who were there, turns off the light and returns to the room he came from originally, shutting the door behind him.

Meanwhile, a young boy has pulled the boat behind his boat back to the temple. He moors the boat and rows back across the water returning to the fortress-like building. There is an air of secrecy about the building but not of evil. The view from the front of the building is across an expanse of water to the temple which glimmers gold in the night and stillness. From the promontory in front of the stone building the night panorama is beautiful. It feels as if one can see to the West and see doorways or panels built into a third hill which somehow connects to the other two. Stillness and calm settle over the scene and all is quiet.

SASUHANA

When the leaves of fall leave the trees, I flee my mountain home. The winter cold would seal my doom. Away to the south I go. Spring finds me wending my way north again to the land I love above all earthly planes. In the mountains I feel the glory and magnitude of God as in no other land. Spires of blue, lavender, green breaking against the sky remind me of the cathedrals of heavenly proportions. Here on earth we search in vain for the heavenly appointments. Only in imagination may be behold the wonder of the heaven.

My name is Sasuhana (Saw-sue-haw-na) and I lived many, many years ago, long before the Indian walked the forest floor with quiet stealth. My people were tall, blond, blue-eyed, and fair. We had memory and history of the planets and skies. Our people had come from the planet of ice many years before. They came in haste and without proper preparation because, then as now, they would not listen until the signs were so powerful that they had no choice but to prepare to leave. In our legends and memories lies the story of the planet which turned to ice. A once verdant, lush planet that supported life for millions of people and animals. The end was predicted for generations, but, foolishly, no one would listen. They said, "It was predicted long ago and didn't happen. It won't happen now. Wait. Don't be foolish. You don't want to look silly when the things predicted don't happen." Warnings were ignored in disbelief until the sun began to dim. Even the most foolish then could see what was happening as the world cooled and animals and plants, dependent on heat for life, died away. When the final flash came and the sun flared then died, it was too late to do anything except send the elect, the chosen, those with purpose. It had been hoped that more could be sent but unnecessary and foolish delays prevented this happening.

Today we guard the ancient ways, the paths and the edifices. Since the change, the weather is cold in the mountains and we must leave for the winter months. We do not have means to keep warm and keep the edifices warm. We cannot all stay underground, so we move southward before cold weather. Our bodies are not well adapted to cold weather. The ancient memories are too recent with us. Fall brings a sadness and pain which cannot be endured. We carry the memory of the homeland, although it has been such a very long time since the ships came to earth.

Many were lost after the landing. The earth was not hospitable to the beautiful, fair people who knew nothing of war and fighting. They were unable to deal with the cruelty of the inhabitants of earth. Ours was a fair and generous group. Life and pleasure were based on love and forgiveness rather than war and destruction. Many of the key people were lost before the children could be taught what they needed to know. In the rush, both here and there, the knowledge was preserved, but the wisdom became distorted and lost. Hardship and fear further affected the survivors and again they lost wisdom and some knowledge.

We went into the tunnels to hide the knowledge so that it would not fall into the hands of the unwise. Too much danger lies in allowing the knowledge in among those who do not understand and use it properly. You saw Mynon. He helped to bury the treasures. He was one of the wise ones. He was telling you how hard it was to work at hiding the secrets where there were those who wanted to keep them and use them unwisely. He hid during the dark of night, entering the hidden caves and tunnels while the rest of the group slept. Even then there were those who tried to find where he went and how he hid the treasures. He was very skillful and hid the secrets well. Much anger arose among those who would keep the secrets and exploit them.

Mynon was never safe. He was watched and followed constantly, so had to be very careful. The secrets of the ancients had come to him through the Fathers and were to be preserved and used only by the wise who would use them properly.

THE LITTLE SISTERS PRAISE GOD

Just as the sun comes over the mountain, we raise our hands to God and sing a song of the earth, the sky, the universe. We praise God in all we do. We live the message of God's hope and promise. As we stand with hands uplifted, eyes toward the heavens, and ears attuned to the cosmic songs, we give ourselves to God in total submission and repentance. Only through total submission to the One and Only can we feel his loving presence. Earthly clamor fades away, the tensions release and we are one with the Universal Life Force. Our bodies sing the music of the spheres and we vibrate on the same resonating note of the earth and skies. Mother Earth lends us her strength and grace, Father Time stands still in the glory of the dawning sun. The dawning sun which brings life and hope to the earth.

We gaze at the sun with rapture, drinking in the beauty and absorbing the warming rays. Healing of body, mind, and soul come with the first rays of dawn. Healing and energy for the tasks of the day. We stand with arms uplifted, submitting to the Great Creator and drinking in the rays of the sun with every pore and atom of our beings. No, we do not worship the sun. We worship the Great Love and Creator of the Universe. The One who cared for us and restored us to the rays of healing light. Darkness fades before the dawning light, just as darkness fades in the light of the God who gave us all.

At noonday we stop again to turn our faces to God and raise our hands to him, thanking Him for the day and the lives we so

63

enjoy. Again, we drink in the healing rays of the sun. The sun given by God. As we receive the light, we again feel the energy flowing through our bodies, our minds, our very souls, healing and renewing. God cares so much that he gave the sun to light our lives and to give us meaning. As we return to our tasks, we carry the light and warmth with us, imbuing all we touch with radiance.

The evening sun, glowing crimson on the horizon, hangs like a mammoth jewel in the sky. As we raise our hands once again, we hear the voice of God saying, "Well done My children. Your day has been well spent. Rest and renew, for tomorrow you will start anew." The warmth permeates our very beings, relaxing and calming the wearied soul.

SONG OF PRAISE

Oh, how great and marvelous is Our Father
The maker of us all.
He has given us the precious gift of life.
He has breathed into us the essence of His love.
He has set us on a course which time alone can alter.
He loves us when we falter.
He loves us when we run with glee.

The rays of the sun reach and touch
The heart of man,
Burning and searing away the hurts and pain.
The light gleams and glows.
The light dreams and grows, Filling every molecule,
Cleansing and rejuvenating.

We thank the God of all for the sun.

Amen

About the Author

Alice May Bookout was born in Clarksburg, West Virginia, and writes about the region she knows with energy and passion.

She received her B.S. degree in Nursing from Alderson-Broaddus College in Philippi, West Virginia, and then went on to receive a Masters of Science in Nursing fron the University of Virginia in Charlottesville and a Doctor of Naturopathy degree from Clayton School of Natural Healing in Birmingham, Alabama.

The author has worked in hospitals, a nursing home and rehabilitation center, and has taught nursing. She and her husband have also served as co-pastors of Shiloh Church of the Brethren. Alice May Bookout was the founder and head therapist of Attitudes Unlimited, Inc. She is presently the founder and owner of Ancient Wisdom Health Center, Inc. in Philippi, WV where she and her husband Gary sell Nature's Sunshine Products (herbs and supplements), health foods, do Iridology and Muscle Resistance Testing, and teach classes on adopting a healthier life style.

Mrs. Bookout lives on a farm near Philippi, West Virginia, with her husband, Gary. They are the parents of five grown children and have seventeen grandchildren.

This is her first published work.